BOLIVIAN WEDDING

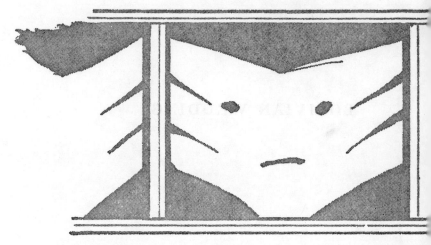

BOLIVIAN

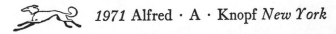

1971 Alfred · A · Knopf New York

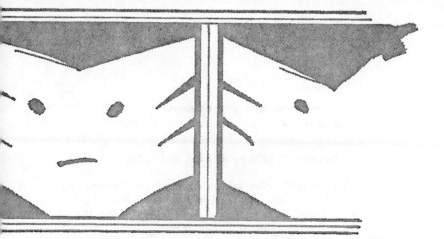

WEDDING

Gudrun Pausewang

Translated from the German by Denver Lindley

THIS IS A BORZOI BOOK
PUBLISHED BY ALFRED A. KNOPF, INC.

Copyright © 1970 by Alfred A. Knopf, Inc.

Library of Congress Catalog Card Number: 72–118717

Manufactured in the United States of America

First American Edition

BOLIVIAN WEDDING

I

A YOUNG FELLOW OF MARGA-MARGA IN BOLIVIA, WHOSE wedding had been arranged for All Souls' Day in 1934, received his draft notice on the eve of that day. He had only two nights and a day before he had to go. Bolivia was at war with Paraguay, and the Bolivian military leaders already suspected there was no longer any chance of winning.

Long before the bridegroom left his shack to join the bride and her family on the church steps, Manuel was groping his way through the village. In the early dawn the contours of the houses slowly sharpened, their façades punctuated by shadow-filled windows. But the streets were still in the dark. The plaza gaped. Above the roofs the sky was paling.

Manuel was cold. His hands slid over walls, doors, fences, reached at times into emptiness and sought a new contact. No sound escaped him. The instant he heard footsteps, he stopped, leaned whistling against a house wall and plunged his hands into his trouser pockets.

"Is that you, Manuel?"

"As you see."

"Up so early?"

"Why not?"

"What are you doing?"

"Just wandering around."

"Can I take you somewhere?"

"What do you mean, take? I can walk by myself. I don't need anyone."

"But after all, you're blind!"

"What's that to you? Go to hell!"

On his way through the village at five o'clock that morning he met only four people. One of them did not know him. Each of the other three offered to guide him. He would angrily refuse, then stand silent until the other, shrugging in embarrassment or indifference, withdrew.

As soon as the footsteps died away, Manuel felt his way onward until finally his hands reached out where there was nothing to touch. Here the village came to an end. The street ran out of the town and into the plain, grew wider and turned into a swath of bumpy wagon tracks. From here on there would be no corral railing, no tree, no wall to guide him. The one clue left would be the ground beneath his feet, and he knew that he must not lose the wagon tracks if he wanted to keep from going astray.

Walking to the cemetery used to take him half an hour. How much time would he need now? Between the last time and today lay the war, the Chaco. Now he was blind. His hand relinquished the rough wall of the last house. He groped into emptiness. His feet felt for the wagon tracks. He found them and forced himself forward step by step, farther and farther away from the village whose early-morning sounds gradually faded behind him. Now and then he was terror-stricken that he might have lost the ruts, that he was wandering at random into the plain where there was nothing to guide him. Each time he leaned over and felt the earth with his hands, until his fingers touched the folds of the tracks. Here no grass grew. They were reliable.

"I've got you," he said aloud. "Yes, I've got you, you ruts. You won't get away from me. Now I've got you for good. I have the trick."

While the eastern sky gradually grew brighter, he groped his way on, whistling. He was whistling a soldiers' song from the Chaco.

What will the people say, he thought proudly, when they find I'm the first one at the cemetery gate? They'll be astonished at the blind man who found his way all alone from the village. They'll refuse to believe it, they'll want to know who guided me. How in the world did you manage it, Manuel, they will say, blind as you are, unable to see the sun or the moon. And yet you found your way here from the village?

I did it all by myself, folks, yes sir, without any damn help from any of you, and there was nothing to it!

He struck out more briskly, for the cold cut his flesh and numbed his hands. Twice he stumbled and fell, but that was nothing, he was used to it, he didn't mind any more. He got up and went on, a strange figure, comical to look at, with his faltering gait and his hands stretched wide in front of his breast.

But what if someone should catch up with me? I don't want that, he thought. I don't want anybody watching me stumbling around like this. How they would stare!

Suddenly he stopped. Wasn't that grass under his feet? But in the wagon tracks there was no grass. In dismay he bent over and felt around. There were no ruts, no crusted folds, no longer a road. He was walking on grass. When had he left the track? How far had he already strayed from it?

His heart beat wildly. He went down on his knees and crawled in a circle on all fours. Perhaps the track was still quite close to him, within an arm's length or two, lost only a moment ago.

He crawled in larger and larger circles, but his knees, his hands, found nothing but coarse grass, and his hope of reaching the road again grew less and less. But how was he to go on from here? He couldn't just stumble on in any direction.

I could sit here and wait until it gets light, he thought. I could crouch right here till the people come streaming out to the cemetery, and then I could wave. I wouldn't even have to wave, they could see me without my signaling, after all, I'm a dark spot and the plain I'm sitting on is yellow. They would come running, they would bend over me and pull me up by the arms and lead me to the cemetery.

You've undertaken too much, Manuel, they would say.

He clenched his teeth and crept on. I'd rather croak, he thought, than have them find me like that.

He beat the earth with his fists. Then he got up and crossed himself.

6 |

"Madonna of Copacabana," he whispered. "Show me the way. I'm not very good yet at this business of being blind."

He crawled straight ahead and in exactly the same direction as the road, which ran not far from him. He came so close that he could have touched the wagon track nearest to him with his outstretched hand. But suddenly the fear seized him that perhaps the morning had already brightened the sky and was revealing him for all to see.

I don't dare either to go on sitting here or to go on creeping, he thought. They must not see me this way! I must walk, walk anywhere, even if it's straight across the plain, just so they won't notice!

It had in fact grown light. The colors of sunrise played across the plain. Manuel huddled close beside the road, breathed on his stiff hands, and reflected. There were still no people nearby, or he would have heard them. But it was quite possible that they were now leaving the town and might soon discover him and his misery, so shamelessly exposed.

So he got up and ran in a direction that carried him away from the road again. Let those who see me think what they like about where I'm going, he thought. So long as I am walking upright, hardly anyone will get the notion of trying to help me. For out here there is nothing I can run into. Here there is only air and earth.

Grass everywhere! He groped his way across the plain toward the horizon. But the Madonna of Copacabana took pity on him, she caused a breeze to blow from the direction of the cemetery. Manuel felt its breath and heard noises. He stopped and listened.

The tin wreaths were rattling!

So the cemetery lay diagonally behind him. Manuel turned around and rushed toward it.

"O Madonna, my life, you have heard me, you have made the wind rattle the tin for me, O Blessed One," he panted. "Just don't leave me in the lurch tonight when I have to get back to the village, will you? Be kind!"

He laughed aloud. They'll be looking for me in the parish house! That stupid fat Brother Pelegrino will be swinging the coffeepot and shouting, Hey Manuel, aren't you up yet? There's work to do!

He imitated the monk, making faces: "Aren't you up yet? There's work to do!" Every morning the same thing. I've always been awake for a long time when he calls, only I never know exactly how late it is. He can't understand that I still have to learn the meaning of sounds, that I have to tell time from the sounds. And suppose I did oversleep—what difference would it make? They haven't any real work for me, these Spaniards, they just pretend to. What would we do without you, Manuel? they say. And I bet they don't even blush when they say it. I peel potatoes and shell peas and clean carrots and wash dishes. Before I was there the monks took turns doing it and it worked all right. Oh, to hell with it, they're always being kind to me. Some day I'll begin to spit at them and I hope I hit them all, in the face, too, only not old Brother Cosme. He's not quite right in the head, he hasn't realized yet that I am blind. Open your eyes! he shouted at me when I bumped into him. And he doesn't bother about me at all. Not him, he's all right. It's the others. The fact that I might be in the cemetery will never occur to them. Aren't you up yet? There's work to do! Pelegrino will be shout-

8 |

ing it right now, and then they'll inquire about me. What? He's in the cemetery? Manuel? Alone? Impossible. After all, he's blind! How can a blind man find the cemetery?

A man lay in front of the cemetery wall rolled in his poncho. He had arrived with his donkey at the cemetery on the eve of All Souls' Day. He was a peddler of funeral wreaths. He had piled them up beside him for the night; now he yawned and squinted from under his poncho into the cold morning light. Suddenly he saw not far from him a youth running toward the cemetery.

He's stumbling more than he's running, thought the peddler in surprise, and sat up. A drunk, and this early in the morning. Damnation, what's he up to? Can't he see that he's heading right for the wall?

Manuel collided with the cemetery wall, behind which the tin was rattling. He cried out, staggered back and put his hands to his forehead, swearing. But with an embarrassed glance in both directions, a glance that was no glance, he fell silent and acted as though nothing had happened. He felt his way back to the wall, along it, and stumbled over the peddler, who had not been able to get free of the poncho in which he was wrapped quickly enough.

"Who's that?" Manuel asked in alarm. He thrust his hands out defensively and in doing so struck the man in the eyes.

"Who do you think it is?" the latter cried angrily and brushed away the tears that spurted from his eyes. "A man who sells wreaths, that's who. Are you drunk?"

"Have you been here long?" Manuel asked in turn.

"Damn it, can't you see that I slept here?"

Now for the first time the peddler, squatting opposite Manuel, noticed the empty eye sockets and understood.

"Did you see me coming?" Manuel cried and thought, I'll beat him up if he saw me hit the wall with my head.

The peddler decided it would be smarter to ignore the incident.

"Do you suppose," he said, "that I have nothing better to do than stare at the sunrise? You woke me when you fell over me. Otherwise I'd still be asleep right now . . ."

Manuel was relieved. He got up and said: "I was half asleep myself. So excuse me. It's cold this morning."

"Yes, it's cold."

"I'm going to the gate. I'll wait there for the others. Are you going too?"

"I've got to load those wreaths there in front of you."

"Well then, see you later," Manuel said, and felt his way as unobtrusively as possible around the pile of wreaths and back to the wall.

A good thing he mentioned the wreaths, Manuel thought, or I'd have fallen over them. This way, he didn't notice a thing.

Poor devil, thought the peddler. Both eyes gone and still so proud. He won't be able to keep that up for long.

As the bridal pair came out of the church the cold wind of the highland struck them. The groom hesitated for a moment on the church steps, while the morning sun threw his shadow and that of his bride against the Roman arch of the doorway. There, carved by an awkward Indian hand, stood a bishop; large-eyed, hollow-cheeked, surrounded by clusters of grapes and ears of corn. Beneath his feet writhed a voluptuous mermaid, waving her scaly tail.

The wedding party pushed the bridal pair down the steps and into the street. There were the two families and a few neighbors. The women surrounded the bride, a brown-haired girl with the eyes of a startled animal; the men grouped themselves with the groom, who was grinning in embarrassment. A llama caravan loaded with dry brushwood moved past the church, separating the two groups, forcing them close to the house fronts and enveloping them in dust and animal smells.

The bride glanced about timidly. At this instant the groom seemed to her very far away. The heads of the llamas fragmented him, brushwood broke up his image, light and shade made it dissolve. She longed for her mother, but beside her stood only her little sister, looking up at her. She seized the girl's arm, pulled her delicate face, her drooping shoulders close to her and giggled in order not to weep.

"You're giggling," said the little one, "just the way you always do when you're afraid."

"Be quiet," said the bride.

"Are you afraid of him? He will be good to you. He will not beat you more than others beat their wives. He gave me an apple. No one has ever given me an apple before, and what a fine one!"

"Right now I would like to be at the stream washing clothes the way we always do on Fridays. Just looking at the stream, with my hands in the cold water, and then spreading the clothes out, and no one there but Carmen and Nena and the Ramirez's little Cecilia and you."

"But everyone has to get married, you know that."

"Yes, of course. But it still feels strange, somehow," the bride sighed.

"If you like," said the little one, "we can run away. But father will beat us."

"No, I can't, I'm grown up now. But you must come and see me often, do you hear? And then I'll take time off and we'll play ball behind the house, all right?"

"Yes," the little girl said solemnly. "You can depend on that."

The bride released her sister and made her way straight through the llama caravan and into the circle of laughing men. She plucked at the groom's arm. He turned around in surprise.

"The musicians aren't here yet," he said.

She remained standing behind him, and when the caravan of llamas had passed the other women also came across and joined the men. Only the crazy one, the groom's sister, stayed on the side next to the church, staring upward. She saw a bird's head dancing on the roof, a gigantic red mask with a gold beak.

The wedding party settled themselves on the ground, stared at those who were already setting out for the cemetery, and waited for the musicians. All of Marga-Marga was afoot!

The bridegroom picked up a straw and put it between his teeth. He was nervous. There sat his bride. He was married, O Madonna! And the people were here on his account, the festival revolved around him!

I will have many children with her, he thought. I will come home from the war and make her proud of me. I will bring her cloth from Paraguay, a pair of patent leather shoes, and a silk blouse. Think of it—a silk blouse!

And his thoughts were already down in Paraguay again, in the courtyard of the villa he had dreamed up, a villa on the shore of a river, surrounded by trees greener than trees ever are in the highland, even in spring.

The doors are open, white curtains billow in the wind, a few folding chairs stand here and there in the courtyard, which is cool under the tall trees. Three men with fishes' bodies spew water into the basin of the fountain. (It was the sort of fountain the rich mine owner in Marga-Marga had in his garden.)

The bride crouched down beside him; her bare feet were scratched and red, but they did not hurt. She had never had a pair of shoes. After all, who had shoes? She had small broad feet with wide-spread toes, and this morning was so cold that she hid them under her skirts.

"What are you thinking about?" she asked.

The groom came back from the marshy river region and looked at her blankly for a moment, then he gave her a slightly twisted smile.

"Oh, nothing," he said.

"About Paraguay?"

"Yes."

He turned away from her and stared nonchalantly at the street.

"He is still young," the aunt of the bride said to the groom's mother and nudged her in the ribs. "He's still shy. Just see how embarrassed he gets when she speaks to him. He's probably never had a girl."

"He's a good boy," the mother said earnestly, "and he

will get used to her. She is good too. She can work and she's not too smart. We chose her for him. He will be pleased with her and she with him."

The bird's head was dancing in front of the glaring white of the church façade, appearing and disappearing. Now it was grinning from the belfry. The crazy girl pointed upward, but her mother saw nothing. When the girl called to it, it shrank, shot downward in a series of mad capers and lay down in her lap. In astonishment she stroked its feathers and gold beak, and it began to coo sleepily.

"Paraguay?" the bride asked. "Is it the same as here?"

The groom did not immediately understand what she said, for the wedding party were all talking at once in loud voices. Chickens cackled among the bundles, twitching their fettered legs. Children romped among baskets and jugs.

She repeated her question and moved closer to him.

"Paraguay is down, and we are up," the groom replied. "In Paraguay there is forest everywhere and in it are birds with bright-colored tails, and butterflies and monkeys. And there are flowers as big as your face. They climb on long stems into the trees. The grains of corn are as big as nuts, and there is a harvest four times a year. It is so warm that you don't need a poncho."

"You have never been there," the bride said, "and still you know what it's like. You are very clever."

"I keep my ears open," the groom replied proudly.

"The people there must be very rich," said one of the bride's brothers, who had been listening.

14 |

"No wonder," cried the second brother, "with grains of corn as big as that!"

"They're supposed to have villas, white villas on the river," the groom said dreamily. "I saw a picture that someone sent, a man who is down there now."

"Do you think there might be a time when you would be allowed to go into a white villa like that?" the bride asked.

"Into the courtyard at least, as far as the fountain," the groom replied.

"What happy people. To live in white villas and have such big flowers and grains of corn. Why do they make war on us?"

"Who knows."

"And if it's such a paradise down there, why does everyone say: Good God, you poor fellow, now you have to go down there too, God have pity on you!"

"It's the Gran Chaco," one of the two brothers replied. "It's supposed to be hell itself."

"Why? After all, it's down there."

"But nobody lives there."

"Tell me more," cried the bride. "I want to know what it's like where all of you will be."

"When I come back, I'll tell you," said the groom. "Then I'll know all about it."

"But so far nobody has come back, only the blind, like Manuel. And the cripples."

"A blind man can't fight any more, that's why he has to come home, although the war isn't over yet, because he would be in the way of the others. But those who are all right stay down there till the end."

"And what if they make you blind too?"

"Manuel didn't watch out. Whoever doesn't watch out gets caught, that's obvious. But I won't set myself up like a target and make big eyes at them so that they can shoot in my face. I'll watch out. I'll stay healthy."

"And what if they kill you?"

"Me?" the groom cried, laughing. "Look at my hands, look at my muscles! Just let them try."

"Yes," the bride said proudly, "you are very strong."

"We were watching when he beat up that big Pepe Hernandez," said the younger brother. "You should have seen that. He won't let anyone come near him."

"But if they shoot?"

"Not all the fellows from Marga-Marga will get killed."

The bride gave him an uncertain look, then lowered her eyes.

"We won't let him out of our sight. We'll crawl along behind him and not spare a single Guarani. We will bring him back to you," said the bride's two brothers, who were also going down into the Chaco.

The musicians had arrived. Everyone got up and with much shouting, gathered up children and baskets and formed a procession that started to leave the village, led by the musicians. One, an old wrinkled flute player, had a cap drawn far down over his ears. His pants were much too big for him, God only knew who had given them to him! The buttons were missing in front, but he had pulled the two sides together and secured them over his hips. It was a good pair of trousers, not to be compared with the rags the guitar player had on. The flutist was a drunkard, as everyone knew, and squandered everything his flute brought in on drink, but he didn't need to feel ashamed in front of the guitar player. That one was given to fits from time to time, full of high-spirits one day, down in the dumps the next, disgusted with everything, beginning with himself. If he hadn't been so penniless, the women would have found him a man to dream about: a guitar player with a hat on top of his woollen cap, a wad of coca in his cheek, black-bearded and devil-may-care. And there was also a pockmarked, wiry-haired drummer, scarcely more than a child, wearing a tattered poncho.

Behind the musicians the bride and bridegroom were dancing. Each danced alone. Sometimes the bride's skirts unfurled like the tail of a peacock, her bare feet skipping on the pavement. The wedding party danced behind her surrounded by yelping dogs. At the very end of the procession trotted the women with children on their backs, and old people.

The bride did not avoid the groom's eyes, but they exchanged not a word on the way to the cemetery. Both knew what was proper, so they did not speak, but now and then they smiled at each other. They still had a day and a night, endless time.

The wedding procession left the town and moved through the treeless plain. Cloud shadows drifted overhead and herds of llamas grazed here and there. The summits of distant mountains glittered, but their slopes were hidden in mist. The plain drew everything toward the horizon: the town, the wagon tracks, the grass. But there, directly in front of them, lay a rolling hill. On its slopes the cemetery clung fast.

So that is where we will spend our last day, the bride thought. She was tired and stopped dancing for a while.

| 17

The crazy girl began hopping about all alone behind the procession. The bird's head hung over the village, its feathers hugely ruffled, watching her with its white eyeballs. The plain whirled around her, the mountains pitched forward, the cemetery tilted. The bird's head drew a fiery red spiral around the circle of the horizon until it burst with a high piercing sound, shedding its feathers all over the plain.

The crazy girl collapsed. Her hat fell back onto her neck, the wiry grass scratched her face.

"Turn around," a woman said to her mother. "There lies your daughter."

The mother dropped out of the procession, hurried back to the crazy girl to lift her up and drag her along. The cemetery was now closer. Ahead of them and behind them moved other groups: single families, whole neighborhoods, masses of children, figures bowed against the wind, barefooted all of them, dusty, ragged. The edges of their ponchos fluttered like wings—long lines of hopping condors. But the women were bright figures. Scarlet, orange, and turquoise, they brought the plain to life with their colors. Even their blacks shimmered with color.

That was the wedding party's road to the cemetery: wiry grass, powdery on the yellow earth, a column of dust, and music.

Manuel was leaning against the gate. Since the early hours he had been smiling at those whose footsteps and voices he heard approaching. A whole day in the cemetery, just like before! he thought. And a fine day too!

"What, are you only just arriving?" he shouted again and again. "I've been here for a long time. I was the first one out of the village. I was here when the sun came up."

"How in the world did you manage it, blind as you are?"

"I got here in a quarter of an hour, and I plan to stay in the cemetery all day and into the night."

"What a man you are, Manuel," people said, clapping him on the shoulder, though they knew that only a galloping horse could cover the distance from Marga-Marga to the cemetery in a quarter of an hour.

They came not from Marga-Marga alone but from neighboring places as well, all those whose dead lay in this cemetery. Five villages belonged to this cemetery: Huapi, San Pablo, Los Haticos, Merengue, and Marga-Marga. Most of the pilgrims came on foot, some on donkeys, the rich on horseback. Only eighteen horses stood outside the gate.

Manuel listened. The esplanade in front of the cemetery had slowly filled with people. Here many peddlers were lined up, hoping for the biggest business of the year. To Manuel's right a man was selling tin wreaths, on the other side of the gate a woman was hawking candles. There were dealers in licorice and pinwheels, a shooting gallery had been set up, a soup kitchen, a lottery with toys. Men were shouting their wares from the booths. Manuel knew the uproar from earlier days. Someone was hawking earthenware. Men gathered around a donkey that was for sale. Among the voices Manuel recognized that of the sacristan from the parish house in Marga-Marga. He was offering religious pictures and amulets. But to Manuel one cry drowned out all the rest—he was hungry.

"Tortillas, tortillas!" shrilled a child.

Is it a boy or a girl? he wondered.

A fragrance drifted over him, awakening memories. That must be Serafina, who worked in Don Leo's store in Huapi; a capable girl, though languid in manner. Her clothes always smelled of soap. She was something special, she wore city dresses and not just on Sundays, and wore her hair in a net. She was not stuck-up but friendly toward everyone who came into the store, and Don Leo knew what a treasure he had in her. The fellows had been crazy about her and had bought combs and shoelaces and licorice from her simply to visit and joke with her, perhaps too in the hope of her agreeing to a secret proposition expressed only by a wink or an unobtrusive touch.

But Serafina did not oblige. She rarely slept with a man, although she must be well over twenty and was getting fat. No more than four names were ever mentioned, and one of them had been Manuel. He thought of that night now as he smelled the fragrance of the soap, a night in the middle of the pampa, on the road from Huapi to Merengue. She had let him take her home and on the way he had suddenly seized her arm and said: "Now we are exactly the same distance from Huapi as from Merengue. Now you will sleep with me. Here on the pampa." And that was when she had begun to unbutton her blouse of her own accord. She had surrendered to him completely, and he had taught her all sorts of things, in the middle of the pampa, on the hard grass, under his poncho in the wind, and for days afterward his poncho had smelled of soap. "Aha!" the fellows had said, sniffing and casting significant glances around. "That devil Manuel, he made it!"

Afterward she had smiled at him from time to time

when he went into the store, and once she had said to him softly: "There's a storm on the pampa today. Will you take me home?"

But for him it was over. He had possessed her once, and then he had found others. He had been a handsome youth, girls had stared after him on the street, and the maids in the Hotel Atahualpa had hated one another because of him.

Now a group of people were moving past him, talking, and there was the smell of Don Leo's soap.

"Serafina?" he asked softly.

There was a rustling in the grass, voices fell silent, then he heard her warm voice: "Yes?"

Footsteps withdrew, the fragrance remained.

"Are you still there?"

"Yes, Manuel."

"Did you recognize me?"

"I haven't seen you since you went into the Chaco. But they told me that your eyes are gone. So I recognized you right away."

"That's not hard."

"No."

They were silent for a while.

"How did you recognize me when I was going by just now?" she asked.

"The soap."

"What soap?"

"You always smell of soap."

"Of soap?"

"Has no one ever told you that?"

"Whom do you mean? My husband?"

"Are you married?"

"I got married after you left. An assistant in Don Leo's store."

"I didn't know that. They just told me you were still with Don Leo."

"That's true. My husband was killed just before you came back. He'd been in the Chaco barely a month when he was killed."

"And now you're back working at Don Leo's?"

"As always. And you are at the parish house?"

"For the time being."

"Can you stand it?"

"I'm indispensable. They can't do without me."

Serafina said nothing.

"They need my advice. After all, I know all the people here. They always consult me before they go to see anyone, because they don't know how it is here, yet. They're from Spain, you know. You—are you there?"

"I'm listening."

"If you like, I'll walk you home tonight across the pampa, to Merengue."

"You?"

"Why not? This morning I walked here all by myself from Marga-Marga. It was nothing."

"No, I'm here with my mother-in-law. We're walking home together."

"As you like," he said and turned away from her.

She gave him a look that was half pitying, half mocking, and walked on into the cemetery.

The strong wind trapped itself in the cemetery, in the corners of the walls, and rattled the tin ornaments beneath the crosses. This was the concert of the dead, wild noises on a cold day.

But Manuel had already heard something else: the lively music of the wedding procession in the distance.

The musicians put their instruments aside and spat on the ground, bride and bridegroom reeled dizzily out of the rhythm of the dance and stumbled exhausted toward the cemetery gate. Manuel heard their feet scraping on the clay. By the music he realized that a bride was approaching. He smiled toward her.

"The bride is beautiful," he said loudly, looking toward where he thought she was. Everyone stared at his empty eye sockets. The bride stopped and blushed.

"Yes," the groom said, "you're quite right. My bride is beautiful."

Manuel laughed in satisfaction. His journey to the cemetery had not been too much to pay for these words.

"Why don't you show me your flowers," he said.

The bride held up her bouquet, but he turned his head in the wrong direction. Then she touched his hand with the flowers. On the way the wind had torn the bouquet so that by now half the blooms were gone, and those that remained were tattered and wilted.

Manuel touched the bouquet. He smelled a delicate, unobtrusive fragrance, a fragrance laden with memories.

"Give it to me," he begged and thrust his head forward to listen.

He heard no answer. Bride and bridegroom looked at each other. She was shaking her head, he was gnawing his lower lip.

"It is for Emilio," said the bride. "I promised the flowers to him."

Manuel gave a harsh laugh. "You intend to beg him for something? He is to watch over your bridegroom, that's it, isn't it? But your man won't come back, and if he does, something will be missing—an arm, a leg, both maybe—or his ears, his eyes . . . You can see how I came back. My mother gave a lot to Emilio. During the time I was away she came to the cemetery at least ten times before she finally died. I'd rather have stayed out there in the Chaco. In a minute it would have been all over, I'd be at peace now. But she got this Emilio to take a hand in the business, so I lost only my eyes. He could tell my mother: Here is your son, back from the war, just as you asked. His eyes? You never mentioned his eyes."

He stepped close to the bride, felt for her arm and squeezed it hard.

"What am I to do now, blind, up here in the highland?" he cried. "Will Emilio tell me that? Is he helping me? Will he give me a living?"

The groom pushed him back.

"Go on, give him your flowers!" Manuel shouted at the bride. "So he'll hear you! So he'll bring your bridegroom back again! He can do that, all right, he can manage it. But to bring him back safe and sound, that's too much for him, too much, do you hear?"

The bride recoiled from him and ran through the gate into the cemetery. The bridegroom and the wedding party followed her in disorder.

"Go on, get lost!" Manuel shouted into empty air. "What are you standing here for? Or do you like looking at me to see exactly how your man will look if he ever comes back from the Gran Chaco?"

He waited.

"Answer me!"

He felt about and realized that he was alone. Only the

24 |

bride's little sister had stayed behind. She stood a safe distance away and watched him open mouthed.

He leaned against the cemetery wall and turned his head this way and that in dumb despair. The child came close and touched him with her fingertips.

He gave a start of alarm and drew back. "Who's that?"

"I'm the bride's sister. Come into the cemetery with me," the child said.

He wanted to burst out in rage, but then he realized that it was a child's voice he had heard. She felt pity for him. Damn the kid, damn her pity. But there was no sense in shouting at her.

"You make fun of me, all of you," he said. "I know you. The kids on the street run after me and laugh when I stumble. Get away from here, you bastard, and leave me in peace!"

"I saw you lots of times but I never bothered you," she said.

"But you glop at me, you glop at my empty eye sockets and you think—how horrible!"

"I do look at where your eyes used to be, but I don't think it's horrible."

He covered his face with his hands.

"Girls don't look at me any more," he said. "I frighten them. No girl will ever marry me."

"In five years I'll be sixteen, then I will marry you," the child said.

He had to laugh, and let his hands drop.

"I believe you because you are still a kid," he said. "You can still really mean it. But in five years you'll be grown up, then you'll think like the others. You'll be laughing at me yourself. You'll be looking at the boys that make the other girls turn around. Marry me? They'd all make fun of you, they'd say you were crazy. No one marries a man like me. What would you get out of it? You'd have to raise the children all by yourself!"

Someone called her. She pretended not to hear and stayed where she was.

"Come along!" The cry came again.

"I'm coming," the child replied.

"Do they mean you?" Manuel asked.

"Yes."

"Why don't you go?"

"I'm going."

He heard no footsteps.

"Hey," he said, "are you still there?"

"I'm still here, but I really am going now. Adiós."

II

THE BRIDE WALKED BESIDE THE GROOM ALONG THE middle path, across the narrow strip where the rich dead lay buried, and entered the section of the poor, which stretched far up the hillside. To the left lay the children under white crosses, to the right the adults under black ones; a white field, a black field; between them the path, and in the exact center of the cemetery the fountain, which never ran dry as the village fountain sometimes did. A fountain with twelve pipes, though its water served no useful purpose here, the flowers being made of tin. More than a hundred years ago, a rich man of Marga-Marga had donated this fountain. One day he had sent his workmen to the cemetery to put it up. Why? No one knew. Was it because the cemetery was such an eerie place? Had he thought that once the fountain was there people would plant flowers? But he had forgotten to donate fertile soil and seeds, so tin flowers were all there was.

More and more people were borne by the wind through the gates and up the slope between the graves.

Infants peered out of their mothers' carrying cloths, dogs wandered around among the crosses, chickens with their legs tied cackled. Today the fountain did not gush in vain. Its twelve pipes were filling up soup pots. What a splendid All Souls' Day! Enjoy yourselves, dead friends!

The people made way for the wedding procession, stopped and peered after it. Two of the poor had been married. And wasn't the bridegroom one of those who had to go away tomorrow? Poor wretch: only one single night for him to enjoy his young wife.

"But what of tomorrow? Don't talk about tomorrow. It's still a long way off."

"Do you see her eight petticoats? Her father spent a lot on this wedding."

"And he's only a tenant farmer himself with no more than a few llamas to his name."

"And the father of the groom?"

"Don't you know him? He works in the mine."

"God have pity on the bridegroom. They say that four more boys from Huapi have fallen, and two from San Pablo. Valerio Ramirez too. Do you remember him?"

"Not Valerio! He was the wildest fellow in all San Pablo. You still remember, don't you, how he cut up at the Zubiaga brothers' wedding?"

"Now he's rotting in the Chaco."

"Do you know why they're having a war down there?"

"No. Do you?"

"It's all explained in the newspapers. But which of us can read?"

"There's nothing to be done about it. It's the government."

"We've got to take it as it comes."

On each of the wooden crosses hangs a tin wreath stamped with flowers and leaves, childishly formed and garishly painted, little ones for the poor, larger ones for those who have laid aside money for their death or who have rich relatives. Some wreaths still shine with bright colors, others have long since faded in sun and wind. Here and there on the mounds of yellow clay lie gifts for the dead, already broken or half weathered away: a jug, decorated with the mask of a grinning god or a puma or the sun. On the children's graves lean clay horses, roosters with huge tails and combs, dolls and birds of clay.

This is all we have, little ones, you know that, don't you?

The wind drops, there is the sound of murmuring, cries, laughter. And at once the wind comes again, sweeps in over the wall, whistles among the wreaths. The tin bangs and screeches, drowning out the voices of the guests on the graves. During the next lull the sounds of murmuring and laughter rise again, until the wind sweeps down once more.

Far back near the wall, among the graves of the nameless, the strangers, lies Emilio's grave. It stands out among the barren mounds of clay, for it is piled high with flowers: Emilio, the intercessor, helps only those who give real flowers. Camomile, clover, furze, even a few geraniums and larkspur are his: a grave with not a single tin wreath, the finest grave in the whole cemetery for the murderer!

The wedding party pushed its way through the crowd. All Marga-Marga was up and stirring, greeting friends from the neighboring towns. Here they all saw one another again after a long year. Brothers embraced, sisters showed each other their children, mothers put questions to their daughters. By the wall the old men got together and haggled. Women squatted by the edge of the middle path, selling tortillas and sheep's cheese. On the graves sat the families. Sometimes it was crowded, for whoever came by was invited to join in. Soup steamed from the little hearths beside the crosses.

Bride and bridegroom moved toward Emilio. The crowd was dense around his grave, flattening the neighboring mounds and pressing against the brick vault, which was no higher than an oven. The rich from Marga-Marga and the nearby towns had adorned it with votive tablets.

Thank you, Emilio, for granting my wish.

Through your intercession, Emilio, I am well again.

With amazement, children fingered the silver hands, eyes, limbs that had been set into the mortar. All these Emilio had healed! But he could do much more than that: he had brought lovers together, caused cold hearts to glow, brought children to the childless, sealed business deals, brought money into the house, changed the weather, made harvests plentiful, prevented fires, saved youngsters from harm, ended epidemics, increased the numbers of sheep and llamas.

But he had to have flowers. Without flowers, his heart simply wasn't in it. The monks of the parish of Marga-Marga adamantly refused to give flowers for Emilio; they said their flowers were grown for the altar, not for a robber. Luckily there was camomile aplenty blooming in the cornfields everywhere. Even clover was acceptable to Emilio. Just as long as they were real flowers!

One day the monks had shown a film in the parish hall, all about nothing but flowers: brilliant-hued gossamer lovelies, stars, suns, all kinds of marvelous shapes. No one had ever seen anything like them growing in the highland soil. Such beauties could be found only in the lowlands, which enjoyed God's special favor.

If only they could deck Emilio's grave with such flowers as those, the people thought. Why, he would joyfully cover the highland with forests, he would make it warm and able to yield four harvests every year. He would let money come raining down on Marga-Marga. Give him a single one of those flowers, flame-colored and the size of a child's head, and he would put an end to the war!

A child laid a bunch of grass on the grave. The grown-ups smiled. Grass! But it was a child and had not been able to find flowers. Emilio had a heart; he would see, of course, that the grass was fresh, plucked at the edge of a stream.

Candles burned in the vault. Now and then someone in the crowd bent down, lit another candle and added it to the array. The wind could not reach the flames. Tiny threads of smoke rose and were swept away, along with the murmur of prayers, in the storm.

Everyone knew that Emilio had been a robber, but he had never killed anyone. He was innocent, though they had tried to convict him of a triple murder. He had stolen quite a lot, but dear God, who wouldn't do that with the water up to his chin? It was always only the rich he had robbed, in the neighboring towns, never the poor of

Marga-Marga and thereabouts. Proof enough that he was a good man! And a smart one, too! They never caught him. They could prove nothing against him.

Until that morning when three corpses had been found in a nearby town, in the house of a lawyer who had gone away for a few days: the lawyer's handyman, his maid, and a nine-year-old girl whom the lawyer had bought from a beggar woman some time before and who had become the maid's helper.

All the drawers in the lawyer's house had been ransacked, papers strewn everywhere. But the killer had taken nothing but money; a lot of money, they said, which did not even belong to the lawyer.

Emilio's house was searched at once and a bloody knife was found, but not the money. Emilio was working in his field when the gendarmes arrived. He did not merely pretend to be amazed, he really was. He insisted that he knew nothing whatever of the robbery or of the murders. But they had found the bloody knife in his house and that was enough. Before he was shot, they said, he cried out: I am a robber, sure, and I am sorry for that, but I never murdered anyone and certainly not a child!

That strange story was never cleared up. There were those who were sure that the police lieutenant had done it himself, so as to finally convict Emilio, that thorn in his flesh. But for that three murders would hardly have been necessary. Others said that the lawyer had needed to get rid of his maid because she knew too much about him. Then the handyman caught him in the act and so, in the end, he'd had to get rid of the second witness, the child, as well. Afterward he hid the knife in Emilio's house.

A third rumor blamed the crime on a wandering robber who then immediately disappeared from the neighborhood. The knife in Emilio's hut had had nothing to do with the murder, but had been smeared with chicken's blood.

In the court records the guilt was still ascribed to Emilio, but no one believed it. Emilio was an innocent man who had been put to death, and therefore he was assured of God's special benevolence. His pleas were always heard. He interceded for people day and night. That he preferred to do it for real flowers was simply his way. Still, everybody knew that he had once helped an old woman even though he had not been given a single flower.

It was twenty-six years ago that he had been shot and now he, that brown-skinned Indio with the bushy eyebrows, sat with the white angels in paradise and looked out for the people of Marga-Marga, who had no other intercessor but him, apart from the Madonna of Copacabana. She was there for all of northwest Bolivia; her altars stood in every town and city as far south as Sorata. But Emilio belonged only to Marga-Marga, and maybe a little to the four other villages whose dead lay in this cemetery; five villages at the most—and you could take them all in at a glance. Here he knew every single person! It wouldn't be easy for him to forget anyone. With him one was well taken care of. He was only a small saint, but reliable.

The bride pushed her way through the throng. In front of the grave she knelt down and placed on the ground a can half full of water; into this she thrust the stems of her bridal bouquet. Then she pulled and teased the flowers out until they looked like more than they were.

Bring him back safe, Emilio. Please take care that he

is not blinded. Bring him back with everything that belongs to him!

The groom drew a candle from his trouser pocket, lit it and put it in place. He had no flowers, but he was the bridegroom and so he could share in the bridal bouquet.

Manuel groped his way through the gate and into the cemetery. He tried to move in a straight line, for he wanted to get to the fountain and the path led there. But the people shoved and pressed and pushed him aside. He stopped and listened. Wouldn't one be able to hear the water splashing?

No. All sounds were drowned in the noise of the tin wreaths, even the shouts of the hawkers and the barking of the dogs. Manuel moved forward and stepped on a grave. He felt the mound under his feet.

"Hey," someone shouted behind him, "watch where you're going!"

Manuel turned around and groped in the opposite direction. Graves here too. So the path must be there. Now he knew where he was again. He spread his elbows wide, but thrust his hands into his trouser pockets. No one must notice anything. What did it matter, after all, if he bumped into someone occasionally?

A crowd of people from Merengue who had just poured through the gate pushed him along in the direction of the fountain. There it was, the splashing! Pots and kettles rattled, there was the dull clang of jugs bumping together. He ran into a full pitcher and felt the water on his toes. Someone cursed. Cautiously he groped his way up to the wall of the fountain and drank. Then he listened to the noise of the children and the tin wreaths and waited for the bride's little sister.

I could have glass eyes put in, he thought. If only they weren't so expensive. I'd like to have blue eyes like the gringos. If I had blue eyes, the little girl would take me. Not everyone could have her. Perhaps she will come to the fountain to get water? Then she will see me standing here and will speak to me again.

The little one was crouching in the midst of the bridal circle at the grave of the bride's mother. At the dead woman's feet the men were building a fire with dried donkey's dung, which the women had brought along in their bundles. The bridegroom's mother took a kettle and went to the fountain while women quieted their children and the bride polished the tin wreath on the grave and murmured to the mound: "Look, we're here, Mother. I was married today."

The men sat by themselves, gossiping and staring at the teeming throng among the crosses. Now and then one of them stood up, walked over to a friend he had seen, exchanged a few words with him and then came back. The mad girl stumbled after her mother. They made their way over sleeping infants, bundles and jugs, avoiding fires, stepping on graves. They passed six girls who were squatting around a fresh grave, singing and swaying. From time to time one of the mourners broke into a soft giggle. The crazy girl stopped and stared at them. Nearby an old woman was ladling soup out of a kettle.

"So," she said to the crazy one, "you're a poor thing, aren't you?"

The crazy girl was not listening. She was staring at an infant who lay on the ground behind the old woman. He was wrapped in a brightly colored cloth so that only his tiny face was visible. He could not move his arms, they were held tight to his sides. A dog stole up and licked his face. The crazy girl pointed and babbled, but no one paid her any attention, neither the girls nor the old woman stirring the soup. Finally the crazy girl drove the dog away with a kick, touched the baby and babbled tenderly.

"I can see that you'd like something like that too, wouldn't you?" the old woman said, with a glance at the yelping dog. "But who would marry you? At best someone who wasn't right in the head either. And if no one of that sort can be found, then some night a man may come along who wants to have a bit of fun with you, simply because he can't find anyone else just then. When that happens, just be quiet, you hear, because that's better than nothing at all."

She handed a dish of soup to the crazy girl who accepted it and looked about proudly for her mother. But all she saw was strange faces and strange backs, all strangers sitting on the graves. Terrified, she dropped the dish and ran away. She plunged over grave crosses and children, stumbled over dogs. Her hat rolled off. Round about her the cemetery grew gigantic. She whimpered, but she was too crazed to say the word "mother," and no one knew what she was crying about. Finally she threw herself on the ground and howled aloud.

Children gathered around her and watched her curiously. They began to laugh when the crazy girl picked up pieces of clay and stones and angrily threw them at her tormentors. A little boy poked her in the back with a stick, and when she reached for it he prodded her so hard that she screamed with pain. But her cry was lost in the shrill rattling of the tin wreaths in the wind.

The children hooted. They called to other children nearby.

"Come here!" they shouted. "Here's something worth watching!"

A few of them ran off to look for sticks or poles, for the game with the crazy one promised to be lively.

A couple of women drove the children away and tried to pick up the little girl. But she scratched and bit, beside herself with fear. Then someone recognized her and called the mother over from the fountain.

When the crazy girl saw her mother coming she leaped up, ran and threw herself so violently against her that she knocked the old woman to the ground. The kettle rolled noisily against a grave cross. The crazy girl pressed her face against her mother's and held the old woman's body to the ground.

"You monster," her mother panted. "What more do you want—can't you see that I'm here?"

She had trouble getting back to her feet.

"Now come along, you," she said, taking the girl by the hand. "Sometimes she acts crazier than she is," she said loudly to the onlookers. "But she isn't as crazy as all that. She can even sing. She sings the national anthem note for note, you can easily recognize the song, even without the words. Anyone who can sing the national anthem can't be completely crazy. Her brother taught it to her—day after day he sang it for her until she knew it. She is teachable. And the midwife said that something like this can be outgrown, that it can disappear with age . . ."

She looked around, waiting for some kind of response. She was prepared for arguments, but no one felt like replying. They were all silent, looking at the crazy girl.

"Just wait," the mother said, "in a couple of years she'll be just like anyone else! Anyone who doesn't believe it can go and ask the midwife!"

Even on the way back to the fountain the girl still clung anxiously to her arm.

"Where's your hat?" her mother asked.

The girl was sobbing quietly to herself and did not understand.

"Your hat!"

The mother laid her hand on her daughter's head.

Now the crazy one understood, felt around on her head, looked around herself and shrugged her shoulders.

Her mother searched for the hat, asked the people sitting nearby, and peered behind bundles and baskets. But the hat wasn't there. There was no time to look through the whole cemetery. The fire had already been burning for some time on the grave of the bride's mother, and she had to hurry back with the kettleful of water from the fountain.

"Let me go," she said to her daughter. "You're hanging on me like a sack. You're a punishment from God, and your hat wasn't even two years old. Where are we to find it? Where shall we get a new one? Can't you try to be a little less crazy, so that at least you can look after your own hat?"

She put her arm around the girl's shoulders and patted her tenderly.

The wind blew the hat through the candle smoke on Emilio's grave and from there rolled it against the wall.

"Catch it, catch it!" some children shouted.

But the wind drove it away from them straight across the field of crosses and finally sailed it far downhill near the entrance, into a newly dug pit among the graves of the rich.

The blind man was still standing by the fountain. He heard the water splashing in the mother's kettle, stared with his empty eyes in the direction of the sound. He did not know that he was staring straight at the crazy one, who was pressing close to her mother.

Never had she seen such eyes. The dead glance, fixed motionless upon her, terrified her. She gave a shrill cry of fear.

"Be still," her mother said, without looking up.

The crazy girl pulled at her sleeve.

"Yes, I'm still here."

But that look, that look! Manuel stared in the direction from which the sounds came. Who had made that cry? Who was that, panting like an animal?

At that moment her fist struck him. She hit him squarely in the face.

Manuel, unprepared for the blow, reeled and lifted his hands to defend himself. The mother let go of the kettle and boxed her daughter's ears.

"It was the crazy girl," the people said, trying to comfort Manuel. "She doesn't know what she's doing."

But Manuel was deeply hurt.

"Liars, all of you!" he shrieked. "You can tell me whatever you like, and I have to believe it! You're only trying to protect her!"

"Her mother has punished her," the people answered.

Someone tried to lead him away, but he struck about

him with his fists and would not allow anyone to help him.

"No one has ever struck me without paying double for it! I'll beat her to a pulp!" he shouted.

"Be reasonable," a man said. "What good will it do to beat a poor creature like that?"

"What have I done to her? Nothing!"

"You stared at her."

"And for that she strikes me?"

"If you could see yourself, I bet you wouldn't be able to take it either, and you aren't even crazy!" the man said.

Manuel leaped up, about to shout something more, but suddenly he let his head drop. He fumbled his way through the rows of graves till he reached the wall. There he sank down and covered his face with his hands.

A few people who knew him had followed. Of course, a woman had hit him, that was hard to take. But what could one do? Helplessly they went away again. His wretchedness seemed too great for any comfort.

The mother filled her kettle, took the crazy girl by the hand, and, dragging her along, returned to the wedding circle. There she pushed her daughter between her husband and the bridegroom and said, "Hold onto her if she tries to get away. She has been making trouble. The people will get annoyed at us for bringing her."

The father put his arm around his daughter. She leaned against him and instantly went to sleep.

"She hit Manuel in the face," the mother whispered. "He got very angry."

The man looked in distress at his sleeping daughter.

"Maybe we ought to invite him for soup," he said.

The mother went away and came back. "He says he won't accept charity."

Then the father gently placed his daughter in the bridegroom's arms, stood up and went over to Manuel.

The crazy one gave a few low grunts of pleasure. She snuggled against her brother and gently felt his face with her hands. She pulled at the lobe of one ear and sucked his fingers.

"Same old story," the bridegroom said. "Why do you have to annoy people?" He stroked her hair, and with his other hand kept her hands quiet. She soon fell asleep again.

"She's like a dog," the bride said. "She licked you the way the dogs do."

"She knows me," the bridegroom replied. "She likes me."

Their father seated himself beside Manuel and spoke to him by name, for he had known him well in earlier days when he was still one of the handsomest youths in Marga-Marga and was a waiter in the Atahualpa, the village's single hotel. In those days, the father thought, he would hardly have dreamed that one day Manuel would be reduced to living in a shed at the parish house and doing what work a blind man could manage in order to get food from the monks.

"I'd like to ask you a favor, Manuel," he said.

"Why in hell can't you leave me in peace?" Manuel growled. "I'm fed up with you, all of you. I won't do a favor for anyone. You disgust me."

"It's not a favor that you need eyes for. Tomorrow my son has to go down to the Chaco. You were there for two whole years, so you know all about it. Tell us about it, because we want to know what it's like in the place they're sending our son to."

"Let the priest tell you what it's like in hell, then you'll know."

"Don't make fun of us, Manuel. I have never been out of Marga-Marga. How should I know about the Chaco? And the people tell so many stories that you don't know what is true. You're the only man from Marga-Marga who has come back so far. No one else can tell us about it but you."

"I'll tell you the truth, and it will make you sick."

"You needn't tell absolutely everything."

"Everything or nothing. I don't cheat."

"His mother is here."

"I'm coming," Manuel said proudly and got up. "I'll tell you about the Chaco, all right, and when I do you will know everything, you'll be able to imagine exactly what will happen to your son down there."

The man put his hand unobtrusively under Manuel's arm and led him toward the circle of wedding guests.

"But think of his wife, do you hear, and his mother," he whispered.

Manuel pretended not to hear.

The bride's little sister looked up in astonishment as the blind man felt his way past her. He sat down with dignity, for he sensed that all were looking at him in anticipation, and he enjoyed it.

"Don't make so much noise with that kettle," said the father of the bride.

"Who are you?" Manuel asked.

"People from Marga-Marga," the bride's father replied. He said nothing more, for he remembered the bride's heated words and his daughter's fists. He did not want to arouse Manuel's anger again. If he knew who we are, he thought, he would jump up and run off and who knows, he might strike out and upset the kettle.

"Keep those children quiet," he shouted to the women. "Manuel is now going to tell us about the Gran Chaco."

THE BRIDE'S SMALL SISTER HAD PROPPED HER CHIN IN her hands and fixed her big eyes on Manuel.

"And when we got down there into the lowland," said the blind man, "some of us were already sick, and in the next few days there were more. They just lay there stretched out on the ground. There we were more than three thousand meters lower than here. We could hardly breathe. The heat drove us mad."

A baby began to whimper. Manuel fell silent and waited. The infant's mother, a very young Indian woman, blushed, because she felt that everyone was staring at her child. She got up quickly and disappeared among the crosses where she fell to cradling the infant in her arms, kissing it vigorously to quiet it, for her husband too was in the Chaco and she did not want to miss a word of Manuel's report.

"Walk barefoot? Out of the question. We might as well have tried to run over hot coals. And the mosquitoes! After a few days we saw swarms of them where there weren't any, and we fanned our faces with our hands from morning till night. We got skin ulcers. The sores burst and made us miserable walking, sitting, lying down. We thought only about water, we dreamed about water, talked about water. Every bit of work was too much for us. Even our rifles felt like lead. And the snakes: you don't see them, they're the color of grass, of leaves, of bark. You don't notice them until they're hanging from your toe or your finger, and there are even some that drop from the limbs of trees when you walk underneath."

The bridegroom's mother looked anxiously at her son.

"One night an officer had to get up out of his hammock. He bent over and reached for his boots, but a snake had crept into one of them during the night. It struck him and just happened to hit him in the jugular vein. We killed the creature, but there was no way to help the man. In about half an hour he was dead. From then on we didn't take our shoes off day or night."

"There are snakes up here too, what does that matter?" the bridegroom said. "Once I killed one myself."

"But only nonpoisonous ones," his mother whispered.

"What do you know about the snakes down there," Manuel shouted, "and about all the other things that wait for you down there? Even the men from the lowland, from Santa Cruz de la Sierra, from Trinidad and Riberalta, whose homeland it was, cursed the Chaco and said that it wasn't as bad as that where they lived. But the men from around here just staggered on with their heads hanging like corn during a drought. We hardly ate, we never spoke. Even before we reached the front eight of our company had died.

"Only one man stayed healthy, a little fellow from

Oruro, but he came originally from Cochabamba which lies at a moderate altitude. He looked after everything, saw to our water, kept our rifles in working order and hit us when we wanted to let ourselves drop. Once when nearly all of us were down with the fever, he looked after our food, fetched water, made tea, drove away the snakes and buried the dead, all by himself. His name is José Ribera, perhaps he's still alive. We named him Choclo."

The young mother slipped back and sank down silently among the women. Her baby had fallen asleep, it hung at her breast in a cloth. She listened with open mouth.

"And the cries of the animals in the bush: screeching, hissing, whistling, chirping—you felt surrounded day and night but you saw nothing. You wanted to keep turning around all the time to protect your back."

"And the people down there in the Chaco? Weren't they friendly toward you?" the groom's mother asked.

"Hardly anyone lives there. Only a few wild men who hid from us. I got a look at them only once."

The bride, who was huddled beside the groom's mother, suddenly straightened up.

"I don't want to hear all this," she said.

"Be quiet," her father whispered.

"I don't want to know about it!" she said. "Why do I have to know about it? We have only one more day. And I don't want to spend it all worrying about him."

Manuel thrust out his chin, straining his ears in her direction.

"Oh yes, the women," he said. "They stay at home and are safe. But if you come home the way I am, then they avoid you."

He stood up.

"What are you doing, Manuel?" asked the bride's father. "Tell us more!"

"I'm leaving," Manuel answered, and stumbled toward the kettle, which was hanging over the fire.

The bride's father sprang up and laid his hands on Manuel's shoulder. "Ask him to stay," he cried to his daughter.

"Take your filthy hands off me!" Manuel shouted.

"Stay where you are, Manuel, you'll upset the kettle."

"And what if I do? You can't think of anything beyond your kettle, and if you hear the truth about the Chaco, then you put your hands to your ears."

"Sit down again, Manuel," the groom's father said. "We're not holding our ears. We want to hear more."

"She has to ask me herself, the one who just said she didn't want to hear any more."

The bride stared at him darkly.

"Let him go on talking," the bridegroom whispered to her. "It's probably not as bad as he makes out. After all we can't send him away now."

"Go on talking," she said crossly.

Manuel sat down again and waited for the whispering of the women to subside.

We were encamped on the bank of a river. It was the rainy season, the river was swollen. The Guaranis were camped on the opposite bank. We could see them plainly. But they had no desire to fight that day, nor had we. A lot of our men were wounded or sick. Toward evening when it was very quiet we heard the sound of paddles. We peered out of the underbrush, our rifles at the ready, for we thought an enemy patrol was coming downstream. But we saw that the Guaranis were doing exactly the same. Then we suspected that perhaps it was one of our own patrols. How were we to know who controlled the upper part of the river, they or we?

It was neither our men nor theirs, but savages. They came down the river in a long canoe, about twenty people; men, women, and children, all naked. Their hair hung down in front of their eyes. They wore necklaces of teeth around their necks. Our sick crawled up and peered through the branches, and those on the opposite shore were peering too. None of us had ever seen anything like them. They looked almost like animals.

Everything was so peaceful that evening. Their bodies gleamed red in the sun. The men carried bows and held quivers between their knees. Children laughed. One of the women was trying to quiet them. There were girls among them too, but I tell you, they looked like monkeys.

Suddenly one of them discovered us. He gave a warning shout. Paddles were reversed, and then it began. Our officer shot first. We fired at almost the same time as those on the other bank. The savages wanted to turn their boat around but those in the front of the boat had already fallen into the water. The women leaped up screaming shrilly, the canoe upset. We saw their heads moving in the water and went on shooting, although we could not distinguish the men from the women. We could tell the children only by their smaller heads. But they went under almost immediately.

Two women managed to reach the shore on our side. Our officer forbade us to shoot. We let them creep up, but one of them was hit in the back by a bullet. It was a bullet fired from the opposite bank. She fell like a sack. We were furious. The Guaranis begrudged us even the women.

The last one, a quite young girl, made it all the way up to us, but when she saw us crouching in the underbrush she tried to run back down to the river. We caught her. Two of us were shot doing it. We took her to the officer, who pulled her back some distance into the woods, for they were firing at us furiously from the opposite shore. They were jealous. Late in the evening they quieted down. We thought they were tired, as we were, but around midnight they secretly swam across the river, strangled both our sentries, killed our sick with the butts of their rifles, and also found the lieutenant, who stared into their flashlights stupid and drunk with sleep. But when they tried to catch the savage she escaped from them and got away, simply disappeared without a trace. They shot the lieutenant and searched about in the underbrush for a while. We were deadly afraid, because we had rushed helter-skelter into this very patch of underbrush when the slaughter started, and were still hiding there, without weapons, of course. They found one of us too, and in a rage that the wild woman had escaped, they proceeded to have some fun with him. They threw him into the river, pushed him out into the current with long branches and shouted to him: "Swim, Inca, swim!" But what highlander knows how to swim? They knew that perfectly well, of course. He cried for help a few times, then the current carried him away.

"And you?" asked the bride's small sister.

Manuel paused. Didn't he know that voice?

"Toward morning when the others were asleep, I crept

out of the underbrush and made my way back through the woods to try to find our troops. I lost my way, though, and came out on the river again. Finally I found another man who had survived, and then a second. Now two of us could sleep at night while one kept watch. After three days we found one of our units and reported in, half dead from hunger. . . ."

The bride's voice interrupted, speaking to her husband: "Didn't you tell me it was a paradise down there, with four harvests a year?"

"Are you asking me?" Manuel cried.

"She's asking me," the groom answered.

"Answer me!" said the bride.

"But it's true," the groom said, "that down there flowers grow as big as a child's head. I heard it myself from a man of Huapi who had been there. He saw them and smelled them."

"What good do flowers do you?" Manuel asked, "if you croak lying among them? One instant you're smelling them and the next you're gaping at them without recognizing them, because there's a knife between your ribs or a bullet smashed into your skull!"

The groom was silent.

"It's hell," Manuel said.

"I'm eighteen years old," the groom replied, "and I'm really pretty strong. I've almost never been sick, only once or twice as a child. I don't think that a man can die just like that, from one day to the next. In any case I won't give up if I get to the lowland, for I can stand a good deal. I will get to Paraguay, to where they have their haciendas and their cities, beyond the Gran Chaco, and I'll see all those marvelous things with my own eyes."

"That's right, you'll do it," cried the bride. "You are big and strong, you'll strike them down, and they'll all be scared of you and you'll drive them ahead of you until you see it all with your own eyes!"

Manuel burst out laughing.

The bride's two brothers grinned in embarrassment. They glanced back and forth from the bridal pair to Manuel. But what was there to say? They would certainly do everything they could to stay alive, and certainly not everyone down there would lose his eyes. Manuel had had bad luck. But they stayed silent and fell to scratching pictures of flowers and crosses in the clay mound of the grave on which they were sitting.

The tin rattled noisily, the whole cemetery resounded with tinny clanging, the wind had driven tatters of mist across the wall and veiled the sky in white. The sun was smothered. It grew colder. The din of the wreaths increased. Manuel had to shout.

"You will never set foot in Paraguay! The Paraguayos have invaded Bolivia, for the Gran Chaco is Bolivian, and they will drive us farther and farther back until we have to hide somewhere here in the highland!"

"What you say makes me laugh," shouted one of the brothers. "We keep hearing about our victories and yet we won't set foot in Paraguay?"

"The war is already lost," Manuel said. "And you can go down there and let yourselves be driven back by the Guaranis until you fall dead. Then you will have died for Bolivia, but what good does that do Bolivia? None. And you get nothing out of it either, or perhaps you would enjoy rotting in the Chaco?"

"You're angry at the whole world," the bride said.

"Yes, I am, for it owes me a debt it can never pay. And that is why I'll now tell you how I lost my eyes. I'll tell every single bit of the story so that it will hurt you."

"No," cried the bridegroom's mother, "we've already heard enough. We know about the Chaco. Pablo will not lose his eyes, so we don't need your story. Eat your soup and go."

"I won't go until you've heard my story," Manuel replied. "You're afraid of it, you'd rather put your hands to your ears—"

"Oh ho!" the brothers cried.

"—and go on believing the fine stories the speechmakers tell you in the Marga-Marga plaza. I listened to them once and had nothing better to do than to go down into the Chaco and take part. And now I have listened to them again. All lies. They are making fools of you. Maybe they are fooling each other, too, but anyway they are making fools of you. They ought to let someone talk who has been there. Then it would all come out. That's why I'm going to tell you the story about my eyes."

"Show some consideration for the bride," whispered the bride's father. "She doesn't need to know what happened to you."

But Manuel was bursting with rage. "So you're the bridal pair? Then I'll take double pleasure in telling you. You'll hear everything I have to say. You'll dream of it!"

The bride's small sister bent forward, her eyes glittering with expectation.

Yes, she thought, he should tell it, I want to hear it even if it's terrible. I have never heard how one loses his eyes. "Do tell us," she said softly.

"There was a clearing—"

"Stop!" the mother cried, but Manuel paid no attention.

There was a big clearing; it took a good quarter of an hour to cross it. In the middle stood a ruined building, beside it a walled garden. A former missionary station built by the Jesuits. There was even a chapel with a steeple. But now the Guaranis had made an encampment in the ruins. We were supposed to take it, but didn't know how, for there was no cover. Oddly enough there was not a single tree in the clearing, not even bushes, just short-stemmed, sulphur-yellow grass. Our officers were pressed. For some reason this ruin was considered very important for us, perhaps because there was a spring there. But hardly a single one of us was in his right senses. Those of our company who were still alive were suffering from diarrhea and fever. Two of us who were still fairly healthy were chosen. I was one of them.

We were ordered to cross the clearing at night and to climb into the garden from behind. It was surrounded by a crumbling wall of fieldstone, and, from where we were, lay behind the building. Once inside the garden we were supposed to creep up to the main building, find out where the Guaranis were hidden, and destroy as many of them as possible by a surprise attack with hand grenades. The noise of the explosions was to be the signal for the company to attack from the woods.

I hadn't much hope that this could turn out well. Although we knew there were not more than twenty Guaranis at most living in the building, all the odds were clearly on their side. Nonetheless, we crept off in a wide circle through the dry, crackling, thorny woods and out across the clearing, which even in darkness had a sulphur-ous gleam. Night came quickly, before we had crossed the clearing. Our sentries could only hear us, they could no longer see us. Lifting our feet high, we walked like storks. Not far from the wall my companion lost his nerve and bolted, without trying to find cover and not bothering about noise. I dropped to the ground and froze. Now the Guarani sentries must find me, now they were sure to come!

But nothing moved. I debated whether I should turn around but decided to go on, for I hated to think about the distance I had already covered. I forgot my rifle there in the clearing. By the time I noticed this I was already at the wall and did not dare go back.

I pulled myself up on the garden wall and peered over. Behind the house three or four lamps were flickering. I heard voices. I crept into the garden and hid myself in a bush that had a spicy smell. Guaranis were sitting in the courtyard and talking softly. I couldn't understand them, for they were too far away, but I could hear that they were merry.

I made one plan after another and rejected them all. They had posted sentries in the direction of our position, but here in the garden I could not see any. Did they no longer take us seriously? I decided to creep as close as I could, under cover of the bushes, to these men who felt so safe in the ruin and had just begun to eat. Then I could throw my grenades right into their midst. I was just about to start off when something caught hold of my shirt. I thought I was caught on a limb or a thorn, turned around and found myself looking into a man's face.

54 |

It's all over now, I thought. But the face was smiling, and a finger raised to the lips commanded me to be silent. A hand pushed me deep into the bushes, and then both of us were crouching there. He told me in a whisper that he was a Spanish monk who had been doing missionary work in these ruins for three years. But it was hard. The natives had had no Christian teachings since the Jesuits had been driven out. The missionary station had been abandoned ever since the monastery was destroyed two hundred years ago. He had arranged a room for himself in one corner of the main building. The other structures had been razed to the foundations. He used the altar in the chapel; there was no roof, but it did not rain very often. He and another monk had been in the process of getting the natives used to their presence, but now the war had driven the natives out and scattered them. They had crept off somewhere into the forests.

"And the other monk?" I asked.

"He has returned to Asunción."

"Why don't you leave too?" I asked again.

He shook his head.

"I must be here, you see, in case they return. They will surely come back home again from the woods some day. Not all, of course, for many of them were murdered, but there must be someone here to receive the few, don't you understand?"

"And why don't you join them?" I asked, pointing to the Guaranis. "They wouldn't hurt you. After all, they come from Asunción, they were sent here from Paraguay."

"I don't belong there. I'm not on either side. I'm waiting till they move on, then I'll move back into the house."

"But the Bolivians are going to take these ruins this very night!"

"I can wait. I'm not dependent on the garden either. I know the forests around here. I won't be a burden to your people."

"I must go now," I whispered. "The night isn't long."

"What are you planning to do, my son?"

"I'm going to smoke those fellows out."

I laughed softly, took hold of his hand and guided it in the darkness over the hand grenades at my belt. He became agitated.

"Don't do it," he said. "And if you start to do it, I'll shout before you have thrown the first one. Then it will be all over with you."

"But after all, this is war," I whispered excitedly. "In war you're allowed to kill. And if I don't get them first, they'll kill me."

But he couldn't see it. He said he wanted no killing, certainly not here in his parish. Enough blood had already been spilled long ago when the Paulists had attacked the mission. The Paraguayos were just as dear to him as the Bolivians, he was glad to help both, but not in killing each other. I must stay where I was or return to my own men.

We were crouching in the midst of the bushes which were covered with blossoms that had a strong fragrance. The monk was a giant; even squatting, he towered over me.

"They smell good, don't they," he said, bending a twig under my nose. "This is a hibiscus. The Jesuits planted it."

A little later he asked: "Are you hungry, my son?"

I nodded. He drew two oranges from under his cowl.
"These are Jesuit oranges," he said.

I became impatient.

"I must go now," I whispered.

"Where?"

"To get rid of those men. My people back there are waiting."

"You will not go. Not if you intend to kill them."

I got angry, but he said: "What do you suppose they'll do with you if they catch you? They won't rock you in their arms."

I was at a loss. But I stayed. I have always been stubborn. There we were crouching in the bushes, pressed close together, and over in the ruined courtyard one of the men began to play a guitar. They all sang to the music, softly at first, then louder and louder. They must have been heard way back by our own men at their posts. That's how safe they felt. Did they know how wretched things were for us back there in the woods? Was that why they were so carefree? They were singing the same songs our soldiers sing.

"Be careful now and don't start humming or you will give yourself away," the monk whispered.

I didn't have much time left. Soon the moon would rise. Then it would be too late to creep up on them, for the courtyard behind the ruins was large, and there was no cover there.

I counted twelve men. Were there still more inside the ruins? If I couldn't do away with at least half of them at one blow, the rest would still be stronger than our forces.

But I was the monk's prisoner. I tried to slip away, move around to the right, to make my attempt from the other side of the garden. But the monk held me gently but firmly by the arm. He said: "The only way I'll let you go is back. And if you make a circle I'll give you away. I have good eyes."

He showed me something in his hand. "Have you ever seen a caterpillar as big as this?"

I drew my knife without knowing what I intended to do with it.

"You want to stab me, don't you?" the monk said.

"Oh, no, Father, how could I?" I whispered in dismay.

But he had given me an idea.

The men went on singing. The garden was fragrant. Crickets chirped.

If I stab him from behind, he'll cry out, I thought.

"Look, there," whispered the monk and pointed at something.

I could hardly see it, I was thinking so hard. It was a bird that had lighted in our bush. It did not fly away.

Or could I strangle him? But he is bigger and stronger than I am, I thought, and he would rattle.

"Why do you stare at me like that?" the monk asked, smiling.

"I'm not staring at you, Father," I answered, beginning to sweat.

"Did you know that in this mission more than two hundred years ago eleven Jesuits were murdered? They were killed right here in this garden."

"Why do you tell me that?" I asked, scowling.

"Why are you sweating so?" he asked in return.

"I'm not sweating."

The songs, the flowers, the fragrance. This garden

was truly a paradise because it had a fountain and plants from all over the world. I longed to let myself sink back and go to sleep.

"You can lay your head on my lap," the monk said. "I'll wake you up if it is necessary."

"I'm not tired," I said and thought, I must cut his throat from behind, that's my best chance.

"Shall I turn around?" the monk asked.

"Why should you turn around, Father?"

He felt in his pockets.

"I still have a few nuts here," he said, and tried to hand them to me, but I wouldn't hold out my hands. Then he laid the nuts on the ground at my feet and suddenly said very solemnly: "Spare the savages, protect them from the cruelty of the soldiers if you possibly can."

Then he smiled again and said: "If you get into my room, behind the bed—provided it's in the same place— you'll find a loose stone. Pull it out and reach into the wall. There you will find some more nuts. You will need them. You won't get much to eat."

Then he turned around and exposed his back to me. I raised the knife. My hands were shaking. I was as though paralyzed. I could not do it. He waited quite a while, then he whispered: "Didn't you want to stab me?"

"No," I said, "you're dreaming, Father. I was just playing with the knife."

"How well they sing," he whispered and turned to face me again. He laid an ice-cold hand on my arm. I heard my teeth chattering.

"They have beautiful voices. Do you really want to kill them?"

"Yes."

"God have mercy on you," he replied, then turned around and felt inside his cowl again.

"Would you like—" he said and bowed his head.

At that instant I threw myself on him. He made no sound and sank among the leaves when I let go of him.

I put my knife back in my belt and looked down at him. I had shot many men, but I had never before cut anyone's throat. And there was the moon already, climbing up over the tops of the trees. When it struck the clearing it was much too bright to approach the Guaranis without being seen. The cloister courtyard lay in shimmering light. I knew I had lost my nerve, I had used it all up on the monk. I did not even trust myself to leave the bushes where I was cowering. Gradually daylight approached, the singing ceased, the Guaranis disappeared into the ruins.

Now I was all alone with the dead, in the midst of the fragrance, the blossoms, the animal noises. I felt so miserable, so lonesome, that I bent over the monk to listen whether perhaps he was still breathing. But he was dead. I debated whether to creep back to my people, but could not make up my mind to anything, and so I remained crouched there until the sun rose.

Late that morning I started up out of a half sleep. Without knowing it I had been lying on the dead man. There was splashing from the fountain in the courtyard: a Guarani was washing himself. Garden and masonry glittered in the sun, flowers clung to the walls, crowded the courtyard. I myself was huddled in a sea of flowers; around me bloomed bushes, shrubs, and little trees. I had never before seen anything so beautiful as this garden. It seems to me now as though on that day all the beautiful things were trying to say goodby to me, for this was the last day on which I would see. Next day I was blind.

Yes, a heavenly garden. The monk must have cultivated it. All that day I had time to observe the flowers. I picked a blossom from my bush and examined it from all sides. Even today I could describe it to you in complete detail.

The monk had not closed his eyes, they were staring at the sky. I tried to shut them but they kept opening again. They troubled me. I could not keep from looking at them.

Toward midday I grew ravenous. First I ate the oranges, then I remembered the nuts. He had pressed them into the ground with his knees while I was killing him. One after another I dug them up and ate them, along with the sand that clung to them. When they cracked between my teeth I looked over in alarm at the Guaranis, who were cooking in the courtyard and cleaning their weapons. Now they had posted sentries—one in the corner of the garden wall opposite. But he did not see me. I took a twig and brushed the flies off the dead man's face.

When the sun was at its highest, I became very thirsty. I could see nothing but the fountain, but there was no hope of reaching it. It stood in the middle of the courtyard. Soldiers were sitting at its basin. The angel centerpiece, from whose hand the water sprang, was wearing a Paraguayan soldier's cap. I closed my eyes and listened to the splashing and wished for night to come so I could get to the fountain.

In early afternoon, at the hottest and most oppressive time of day, I opened my eyes and saw birds circling above me—vultures. They were making high wide circles, and it seemed to me that I was their target. What could they want with me? I was alive! Surely they knew that. I looked around. Nothing but flowers. Had one of the Guaranis died?

Suddenly my eyes fell on the monk beside me. So that was it. I'd completely forgotten him. But what if the Guaranis noticed and became interested in the carrion? What if the birds alighted? After all, I could not drive them off!

I saw that some of them were already flying lower and that a couple of Guaranis in the courtyard were looking over at them. One reached for his rifle. They began to shoot at the birds. I watched, breathless. I had long since given up what I had tried to do in my first fright—dig a hole for the dead man. After all, I had nothing but the knife and my fingernails. The monk, as I said, was a giant; it would have taken me half a day to dig the hole. Besides, I would have made the bush move. No. I sat still in the bushes and watched the shooting.

If a vulture falls near me, they will come to get him, I thought. Then it will be all over.

One of the soldiers hit. The vulture sailed down and fell straight into the basin of the fountain. The soldiers rushed up and tried to grab the bird, who was beating his wings and spattering water. The Guaranis almost died laughing. One of them struck the vulture with the butt of his gun, but the bird was tough and continued moving for a long while. They dragged him out of the water by his legs and hung him on a hook on the wall of the ruins, head down. He twitched for a while, then he died.

The birds above me disappeared. I breathed more

easily. From a distance they still stared, spying from above the treetops at the forest's edge. But they no longer came close.

Toward evening the dead man began to stink.

It won't last much longer, I thought.

The garden and the ruins began to glow, my skin shimmered red from the blossoms in my bush, on the wall of the chapel the yellow flowers shone. The roof of the chapel was gone, but it still had a magnificent doorway with saints and angels and God the Father at the point of the arch. The evening shadows made everything stand out. The fountain angel was smiling with a red-gold face.

I remembered the nuts in the wall too, but it was the water in the fountain that drove me mad.

My people over there in the woods have had a long wait, I thought. They may think I was killed long ago. They have certainly seen the vultures. They'll be all the more astonished when things break loose tonight.

It was a true evening in paradise. I could hardly bring myself to believe that on this night there would be men lying dead near this garden, under this angel, under the portal of the chapel. All was so peaceful. Twilight came, then the night. The dead man beside me stank. All day I had huddled almost motionless in the bushes. My body ached. When the darkness came I crept away from the monk. He filled me with loathing.

I waited until the Guaranis emerged with their guitar and began to sing. I knew almost all of them now: the fat man, the man with the crooked back, the one who constantly whistled to himself, the lad, who was little more than a child, and the cook. Also the officer and the two noncoms and the various sentries from the corners of the garden. They stirred up the fire and sat down around it. They were singing a song I knew. At that point I crept out of the bush, wormed my way to the edge of the courtyard and at the instant that one of them saw me, drew the pin on the first grenade and threw it into the middle of the circle. I pressed myself close to the ground. It exploded. Splinters flew. One Guarani gave a shrill cry like a woman, but it broke off quickly.

I lifted my head and stared around. Nothing moved. I crawled to the window where I had seen heads peering during the day. The second grenade flew through it. I breathed dust and waited till the noise and the echo died away.

The fire crackled and smoked. Something had fallen into it. There was the stench of burnt flesh. I stumbled over the guitar. Strings shrilled. The sound transfixed me with terror. I threw myself to the ground and awaited attack from the darkness, perhaps only a shot, some sign of life. But it was deathly still. There was only the splashing of the fountain.

I listened in all directions, but when nothing happened I got up and crawled to one of the empty windows in the other wing of the building and threw my last grenade through it. The explosion re-echoed, a shrill cry arose, it came from somewhere in the ruin and was dreadful to hear, but I liked it better than the stillness. Someone inside was quite slowly breathing his last.

I was as though set free. Now I had accomplished my mission, now my people would come. Surely they were already running across the clearing. I went to the fire, seized a brand, and held it high: what I saw was horrible. But then I heard only the splashing of the fountain and felt nothing but thirst. I experienced the whole hellish thirst of that hot day and went to the fountain. No, I rushed to the fountain, and the last thing I saw was the soldier's cap on the head of the angel. Now it sat jauntily over his ear, but during the day it had been tilted down over his eyes. He looked at me, smiled straight into my face, and I held my mouth in the jet of water while I thought, You should go into the building first to see whether it is really smoked out. Where are the sentries? They can't all be dead.

But the water washed all thoughts from my mind. I gulped it with closed eyes, still holding the torch in my hand.

"Don't tell any more," cried the mother, shutting her eyes tight. "I don't want to hear it. Nobody wants to hear it!"

Manuel laughed.

"Yes," he said. "Now we get to it. Don't think that all this makes any difference to me any more. I tell it to myself again and again, I can almost tell it without hurting. I will spare you nothing. Put your hands over your ears if you don't want to hear."

But no one put his hands to his ears. The little one sat bent far forward, no word escaping her. The crazy girl slept peacefully against her father's shoulder.

I drank, until suddenly a shot pierced the stillness and pain tore at my face. I dropped the torch and staggered. I hit the edge of the fountain with my forehead, writhed on the ground, roared with pain and screamed as though for all those who lay on the ground around me. It was suddenly dark, I could not see the torch, not the sparks, I tried to open my eyes but the lids would not obey, I touched my eyes and my fingers sank into pulp.

I refused to believe it, rolled over on my back and stared at the sky. There were no stars.

I lay, I don't know how long, in the monastery court-yard, probably until morning. Perhaps they thought I would die during the night, but I am tough. It was an endless time. Wherever I felt there was blood: on my face, in my hair, on my neck, in my mouth, and still I was not dead. In rage and fear I waited for my people. They should have been there long ago. Where were they? And then I hoped for revenge and some sort of rescue from this darkness.

Instead of that I was suddenly pulled to my feet. They dragged me to the splashing sound and shoved my head under the jet. I tried to resist but they held me fast. The water was marvelously cool.

"Had enough now, boy?" a voice asked me. Someone wiped my face with a rag, or perhaps it was the tail of my own shirt. The wounds began to burn again.

"Caramba, what did you shoot him with?" someone asked. "Why, he's full of holes."

"With the shotgun."

"Shotgun?"

"The one in there that hung over the missionary's bed. Probably he hunted with it. I couldn't find my own gun fast enough."

"Strange. He came over all alone."

"How do you know he was alone?"

"He would have been covered while he was drinking at the fountain. And all night we thought the others would be coming at us in droves, storming out of the bush after that ambush. But nothing happened. Can you explain it?"

"No. But anyway he's done for, for good."

"And now what do we do with him?"

"That's simple: we send him back to his Incas."

"But I'm blind," I stammered. "How will I find the way?"

"That's your business. Tell your comrades they can come now. There are only three able-bodied soldiers and four wounded left. Besides, today we're very busy digging graves."

"Why do you tell him all this?" the other cried angrily.

"Because in his condition he'll never get there. Run, you damn Inca!"

"But where to? I can't see anything!" I screamed.

"You have a knife in your belt. You can end it anytime you've had enough. We won't take that away."

They dragged me through the ruins. I heard their footsteps, felt the coolness of the rooms, then the heat again.

"Keep walking straight ahead," one of them said. "Then you'll be going toward your camp. They will recognize you and won't shoot. If you hurry you'll be there in quarter of an hour."

"Give your friends our greetings," said the other, and a third voice said: "You won't get that far, but greet the little angel for us, the blond one, and don't forget the Lord God." That was probably the sentry.

They gave me a push and I stumbled off, half crazy with pain. I knew that the grass under my feet was sulphur-yellow, that the heavens above were a hard blue, that the thorn bushes around the clearing were olive-colored. I staggered on, head stretched forward, listening for sounds from in front and behind, and finally I dared to call. My comrades must see me now! They must see what state I was in! Why didn't they help me? They had only to call out to give me the right direction.

The grass crackled in the heat, every sound threatened my ears. The clearing wasn't as wide as this. Why hadn't I reached the bushes yet? Why wasn't I being shot at? The Guaranis certainly weren't going to let me get to my own men.

Finally I heard a voice. But in my excitement I could not understand what it was saying.

"Yes," I shouted. "Yes, I'm coming, help me, I'm blind, they shot out my eyes, those fiends!"

"Yes, that we did," the voice replied. "You're running in a circle, you idiot. The forest is behind you. Or do you want to help us bury the dead whose blood is on your hands? We ought to let you stumble into the grave and bury you right here. That's where you belong."

I heard one say one to another: "Shoot him down. I can't go on watching this."

I screamed. I didn't want to die. I turned and stumbled away.

"And what if he does make it?" the voice asked again. "He'll report that there are only three of us left."

"Before he gets out of range we'll shoot him down. But he won't even get that far."

I stumbled on until I heard shots behind me. Then I dropped to the ground and played dead. The sun beat down on me. Once I thought I heard someone coming to get me, but it was vultures. All around me I heard their soft rustling, but I knew that as long as I was alive they would leave me alone. It grew cooler. Hunger tormented me and kept me from sleeping, but that was a good thing, for I needed the darkness to get to safety.

When the air had gotten so cool that I began to shiver, I decided that night must have come. Full of fear that I might be going the wrong way I dragged myself on. I was even more scared of the Guaranis. What if I met them again? What if it was not yet completely dark? What if the moon had already risen?

I do not know how long I stumbled around the clearing, crazed with pain, before someone caught hold of me and dragged me forward.

"Who's that?" I gasped and reached for my knife.

"Leave that alone," he said. "You should have run away like I did. Now you've got your reward."

It was the man who was to have gone with me into the garden.

"You coward," I said. "You miserable coward!"

"Be quiet," he answered. "If they hear you they'll shoot."

"Yes indeed," I screamed. "If we had been together one of us could have kept watch while the other drank!"

He was silent and pulled me into the bushes. Twigs scratched my face.

"Give me water!" I gasped.

"I haven't any."

"And the others? Why didn't they come? I carried out the orders."

"Twenty-four hours later than planned. By that time most of them had died from dysentery. It got the lieutenant. Within a couple of hours it was all over for him. Those who hadn't fallen sick yet ran away because it's contagious. But most of them stayed here, dead or half dead. It's a good thing you can't see. I hid here in the bushes, you know why? I thought they might have seen me run away as we were crawling toward the wall. Of course I could have come back and reported that the orders could not be carried out or something of the sort, but what could I say about you? I didn't know if you were dead or alive, and if they had tried to take the ruins anyway, my lies would have been exposed. They would have shot me. That's why I waited. I hid in the bushes not far from our camp and watched them in their misery, and when the last one had run away I came out and looked for water, but it was already night and I couldn't find any. All I could dig up was some fruit in the provision sacks."

"Fruit?" I cried. "Have you any left?"

He gave me a mango. I smacked my lips and gulped it down.

"I heard your grenades," he said, "but I would have been the only one who could have joined you. I'm a coward and I admit it. I preferred to put leaves on the foreheads of those who were still alive. Ridiculous, I know. But I had to do something. One stuffed the leaves into his mouth. Now they are quiet, but at noon a few were still yammering."

Stench surrounded me. I smelled and listened.

"How many?" I asked.

"Twenty-one, and four more who are still breathing. I wanted the men from the ruins to come over here and catch it. You should have seen the lieutenant—all blue in the face. He was a prominent man in La Paz, and still young. His father is a mine owner. It's said that he volunteered."

I barely heard what he said next, I was letting myself sink to the ground, which was soft and uneven. I wanted only to sleep, to rest, to dream that all this was not true.

"Are you crazy?" he yelled and pulled me up again. "You're letting yourself fall on the corpses like a sack. Is that the way you want to die?"

What happened after that I can hardly remember. He dragged me on for several hours, far through the woods. Once he even gave me water to drink. Then we happened on one of our positions. I did not tell them he had run away. A few days later, I learned, he was killed. A savage shot him through the throat with an arrow.

I was sent to a field hospital. They took care of me until I was well and sent me home. That's all.

"And what happened to those who were still breathing?" the mother asked.

"He didn't want to leave them to the vultures that were already circling over them, nor have them fall into the hands of the Guaranis. Anyway, they were already unconscious. So he strangled them."

The wedding party huddled confused on the grave of the bride's mother and stared at Manuel.

"Is that really true, what you have just told us?" asked the father of the bride. He put his hands on his son's shoulders to give himself courage.

"Do you think my eyes fell out of my head themselves?" Manuel retorted.

"But maybe my sons and son-in-law will be lucky, they have led pious lives, there is nothing they should be punished for."

"What do you know about war? It doesn't ask whether you're treated fairly or not. Let yourselves be led to the slaughterhouse and be butchered there. It's no different."

"You lie, you lie!" the bride shouted. "The Madonna and all the saints and Emilio have abandoned you because you're so wicked! You want the same thing to happen to everyone that happened to you!"

She sprang up and clawed at the blind man. "Go away," she gasped. "Get out of here, I don't want to see your face any more, I don't want to hear your stories!"

"You've heard it already," Manuel said, grinning. "It will follow you the whole day. It's already deep inside you, you won't get rid of it now."

"But it isn't true," cried the bride.

"By the Madonna of Copacabana, it is true. That's how it was. Why are you scratching at me like that?"

"Stop that," her father said. "Be kind to him. Now he must have a dish of soup with us."

"I'm not hungry after that story!" the bride said.

"Forget it," said the bridegroom's mother, though she felt the horror of the story in her bones. "You must have pity on him."

Manuel leaped up.

"To hell with your soup. To hell with all of you, and most of all to hell with your pity. Yes, I lied, it is all quite different in the Gran Chaco, there's an easy chair waiting for everyone, and a servant girl, a pretty one, with a fan in her hand, and the Guaranis shoot with candy canes. They will spoil you there, you recruits; the officers will rock you on their knees and teach you nursery rhymes. And I tore out my eyes myself, I admit it, because they offended me. That's what really happened. Now are you satisfied?"

He stumbled off.

The bride bent over the dishes and plates and plunged the ladle into the soup. Her small sister slipped away. She was pretending to look at the grave crosses, but out of the corner of her eye she was watching Manuel as he stumbled over the graves.

Dogs appeared. They came creeping up from all directions, timid, ugly, ready for flight; emaciated creatures, skeletons covered with mangy skin, lips quivering. Their eyes glittered, followed every movement of the ladle, their ears rose at the sounds of eating, their noses greedily snuffed up the aroma. They lurked everywhere—among the eaters, the bundles, the baskets. When someone threw them a bone, they fought and snarled over it until the strongest carried it off. Retreating before his growls, the rest went back to crouch around the kettle again with dripping mouths, waiting for the next bone, ready to spring. The groom kicked at them, the grandmother beat them with the ladle, the musicians threw lumps of clay at them. But they stayed.

Only when the people on the next grave began to eat did they leave the bridal party, as furtive and hungry as they had come.

"You see, you're hungry after all," the bridegroom said to the bride.

"I can't help it," she replied. "There's still a lot of the day left. And besides, I don't believe him. Nothing like that will happen to you. Not to you!"

IV

MANUEL SMELLED CANDLE SMOKE: SO IT WAS NOT FAR
to Emilio's grave. Just a bit farther up the hill—in that
case he must be quite close to the wall. He felt about with
outstretched arms. There it was, the wall; the comforting,
protective wall. He squatted beside it.

He was pleased with himself. He had shown that he
did not need sympathy, that he was a man, whose danger-
ousness was real even though he was blind.

He laughed aloud. Now they knew his story and
couldn't get rid of it, however much they twisted it.

But how hungry he was! He thought longingly of the
soup. He had eaten nothing since early morning. How
was he to get food? The smell of soup and meat hung over
the whole cemetery.

I can't just go up to any soup kettle and say, I'm
hungry, give me something to eat, he thought. I don't
want gifts, and especially none given from pity. I'll just
have to grit my teeth till tonight!

Footsteps pattered near, a child's footsteps. They

stopped a short distance in front of him. Nothing happened. They did not go away.

"Well?" Manuel asked.

"Where are your eyes?" a very young voice asked.

"They've gone for a walk."

Manuel sensed the child's amazement.

"They wanted to go off by themselves, just like that, alone, without the rest of the man," he explained. "So I let them. There's nothing special about that. They do it often. Don't yours?"

"No. Never."

"Maybe it hasn't occurred to yours yet."

"No, it hasn't."

"Then you're lucky. Once they've been off they always want to go again, and then you sit there and wait for them and it's a nuisance."

"But what if they don't come back?"

"They'll come all right. Their home is with me. In any case, they can't get into other people's faces, they have their own eyes."

"But right now you can't see at all?"

"No. But I don't need to. I sit here and rest. And when they come back they'll tell me what they have seen."

"Do they tell you beforehand where they're going?"

"No, but I believe they're at the fountain. They like to go there. Usually they sit on the pipes and watch the people drawing water."

"But they might fall into the fountain!"

"That wouldn't matter. They know how to swim."

"Swim!"

"When there aren't many people at the fountain they often jump into the water and splash around or lie on the bottom and look up. But not side by side, because that would scare the people and they don't want to do that."

"And how do they get back to you?"

"They roll like marbles."

"But what if they get dirty?"

"Then I shed a few tears and they're clean again."

"But what if someone steps on them by mistake?"

Manuel laughed softly.

"Don't you know that eyes can fly?"

The little boy was spellbound.

"Yes indeed," said Manuel, "like the bees. Sometimes they hover in the air for a while and look around. Today there's such a big crowd in the cemetery. I think they won't try rolling back. Today it will be better to fly."

Now he felt the child's hand on his knee.

"Can I stay here and wait till they come back?"

"Of course."

Manuel felt for the hand on his knee and discovered that it was holding a piece of bread.

"But if I let you watch you must give me your bread."

The boy gave it to him and watched in fascination as he devoured it.

"Sit down next to me and lean against the wall, for it may take a long time until they come back," Manuel said. "It may take until evening. Do you want to wait that long?"

"Yes," the child said, and sat down beside him.

"But if you bring me another piece of bread, I can arrange for them to come back sooner."

The child jumped up and dashed off.

The bride's little sister stood behind a tin cross and watched Manuel. She discovered that he was hungry and she slipped off to the baskets and bundles of the wedding party to steal a couple of tortillas. The members of the party were gathered there, quieting their children, gulping their soup, and they didn't notice. She hid the tortillas under her poncho and ran back to the wall. She walked past Manuel on tiptoe and dropped the cakes in his lap. Then she hid behind a tin cross, but then it came to her that he couldn't see her whether she was behind the cross or in front of it, and she got up again, took a step forward and then stood stock still.

Now he'll be glad, she thought.

Manuel smelled the tortillas and picked up one of them. And already the dogs were approaching. They crept in front of him and watched his hands.

"Was it you who brought these cakes?" Manuel asked and waited for the boy to answer. But there was no answer. He turned his head this way and that, listening.

"Hey," he asked again, "who threw this stuff at me?"

Still no answer—no one was there. So someone going by must have tossed him the tortillas out of pity. In a rage he seized them and hurled them one after the other in a high arc. Instantly the dogs rushed after them. Tears came to the eyes of the bride's small sister.

I should have told him they were from me, then perhaps he wouldn't have thrown them away, she thought.

Before she could move, the dogs had grabbed the tortillas and rushed off with them. She ran after the mongrels, who were slinking away between the crosses, and tried to retrieve the tortillas. Tortillas for dogs! Who ever heard of such a thing!

She picked up lumps of clay and threw them at the dogs. But only hit one. The dogs howled and dropped the tortilla. The others kept running. The one that had dropped his booty wanted it back and kept snapping at it; she drove him off with a kick. The tortilla lay on the ground, she picked it up and blew the dust off. Then she carried it back to the wedding party and surreptitiously stuffed it back into the bundle from which she had taken it.

You miserable curs, she thought, looking around cautiously to see whether any of the wedding party had observed her. You low-down pack of mongrels, eat dirt if you're hungry!

"What are you doing there?" her father asked.

"Nothing, nothing," she cried, hastily sitting down once more among the others.

"Yes, his mother, I knew her," her aunt said.

"So did I," the mother of the bridegroom said. "I saw her sometimes at market and sometimes she went by our place."

"But you didn't talk to her," the aunt said. "She told me everything, from me she had no secrets. I knew her through and through!"

"Whom don't you know?" asked the father of the bride.

"She was a poor wretch, God knows. She came from a village on Lake Titicaca, the daughter of a fisherman, but she wouldn't wait there till her father arranged a marriage. Someone took her to the city and there she found work in Don Eugenio's house. At that time he wasn't more than sixteen and his parents still ran the house. They took her in as a servant girl. She probably wasn't more than eighteen or nineteen herself, and well developed and pretty, and kept herself clean, and so they gave her the room next to Don Eugenio's room, and Don Eugenio's brother, who was a year older, slept across the hall. She was very devoted to Don Eugenio's mother because she had given her work and had never sworn at her, even though in the beginning she didn't know how to use an iron and scorched one of her blouses, and even when she broke a lot of dishes . . ."

"I saw an iron once," the bride said, "in Don Delicio's store. It must be very hard to use one."

"You would never be able to learn how," her aunt replied. "It takes a special knack. I learned to do it, but it wasn't easy."

The girls and young women who were listening nodded and looked at her with awe.

"Don Eugenio's father was good to her too and did not object when his sons went into the kitchen to joke with her, and when one day she informed him hesitantly that they had tried to get into her room at night, he just laughed and said: 'They're still boys at that age. Chin up!' "

"How do you know all this?" asked the bridegroom's mother.

"She told me when I was working in Don Eugenio's house. She took me aside one time and told me all about it, and she also told me that one of the two brothers is Manuel's father. She didn't know which. When Don Eugenio's parents found out she was pregnant they didn't say a single unkind word to her. They thanked her for her services, gave her six months' wages in advance and dismissed her on the same day. She used up the money quickly, for she could not find a new job, pregnant as she was, and then when Manuel was born she had to give him

| 79

to an old woman to keep because no patrona would take her into the house with an infant. Go back to your own home, people told her. But she didn't want to go back to Lake Titicaca, she was devoted to Don Eugenio's house and she found a new job not far from it. There she worked for long years. Don Eugenio's father died, his brother died, his sister married. Only his mother and Aunt Marisol were left. Almost every day she met one of the family. She greeted them politely, but none of them would admit they knew her. On Sundays her patrona gave her the day off, then she went to Manuel and spent the day with him. Once she brought him to the park, there she met Don Eugenio's mother who was walking with some other ladies. She greeted the old lady in a friendly fashion. showed her the child and said: 'There he is. His name is Manuel.' But Don Eugenio's mother just shook her head, shrugged her shoulders, and acted as if she did not know what it was all about.

"When Don Eugenio was transferred to Marga-Marga, she gave up her position in the city and followed him here. At that time Manuel was already nineteen. She went to Don Eugenio's house and asked him if he didn't need a cook. In the meantime, you know, she had learned to be a good cook and had excellent references to show. But he sent her away even though he was looking for a good cook. He pretended he didn't know her. She could not find work—after all, she wasn't from around here—but Manuel was lucky, he was a good waiter. He did what he could for her. A good son."

"That he was," said the bride's father. "It's said that he even bought her a rocking chair before he had to go to the Chaco."

"Yes indeed, I have seen it with my own eyes, a rocking chair in blue and gold with gilded legs. But Manuel was barely off for the Chaco when she had to sell it. She sold it to Don Delicio, who was glad to get it—for a song, what's more—for she had taken very special care of it, she had only sat in it once, and that was on the day that Manuel gave it to her. After that all she would do was give it a little push to make it rock when the neighbors wanted to watch. Aunt Marisol saw it at Don Delicio's and had to have it. At that time I was working in Don Eugenio's house. All day long she talked about nothing but this rocking chair. Don Eugenio did not want to buy it when he learned to whom it had belonged. But Aunt Marisol didn't know, she had no idea, and she nagged until Don Eugenio gave her the money for the chair. I had to fetch it on a wheelbarrow. On the way I met Manuel's mother. When she saw the rocking chair on the wheelbarrow she began to weep and said: 'A sin that I sold it, because Manuel gave it to me. But if it is going to Don Eugenio, it's all right.'

" 'Don't you want to rock in it once more?' I asked her.

" 'Oh no,' she answered. 'I would be ashamed. Anyone might see us here.'

" 'If you like we'll take it behind the old shed, no one will see us there,' I said.

"She nodded, and so I pushed the wheelbarrow behind the old sheds that are on the road to Oruro. There I lifted it off the wheelbarrow, and she sat down in it and rocked back and forth a few times. I wanted to push her so she would rock faster but she said in alarm: 'Not so hard, the gilt might come off the legs. Then what would Don Eugenio say?' 'Don Eugenio is rich,' I answered. 'A little gilt more or less won't matter, it won't ruin him.' But she would not rock any more, she was uneasy. She lifted the rocking chair back on the wheelbarrow and said: 'You must always keep it well dusted. That's what it likes.'

"I promised to and went on. She walked with me for quite a way, and when I got near Don Eugenio's house she stopped and stood looking after me. Later on she told me that sometimes she would go past Don Eugenio's house when the windows were open and listen to the chair squeaking."

"And then suddenly she was gone," said the bridegroom's father. "From one day to the next. I was one of those who helped look for her in the river. The woman she had been walking with along the bank came running and shouted to us. She simply slipped in. The river carried her off to the lowland."

"Now she is dead," said the aunt. "How well some things work out. Just at the right moment she died."

At last Manuel heard the pattering footsteps approaching again. He lifted his head and smiled.

"There's the bread for you," the boy cried and threw the slice onto his knee. "Now call them!"

Manuel chewed and thought it over.

"Sit down," he said, "and give me a chance to eat first."

Good Lord, he thought, how can I get rid of him?

Finally he had an idea. He stood up, took off his poncho and waved it a few times over his head.

"That's the signal," he said. "Now they know that

they have to come back because I need them. They'll be here right away."

The child stared excitedly at the air. But no eyes came flying.

"Perhaps they're lying in the fountain right now," he cried.

"Could you just go over and see?" Manuel asked. "You can understand that I can't leave here without my eyes. If they're lying in the water, chase them out. By now they really have had enough time off. In a couple of minutes I'll signal with my poncho again, then they'll know what's up. After that you'll have to move fast if you want to see how they creep back into my head. They can really fly damn fast."

The child ran off. He had an important mission to perform, you could see it in his face. He forced his way through dogs and people to the fountain and pulled himself onto the edge of the basin. He stared eagerly, trying to see to the bottom, but the water sprayed and whirled and was murky, for the people had been washing their dishes and soup pots in it.

"Lend me your stick a minute," the child said to a bigger boy.

"What for?"

"I think there are two eyes down there."

"What?" the boy asked, his mouth falling open.

"Quick, give it to me, I haven't much time."

"Has something been slaughtered?"

"Human eyes," the small one answered proudly, "real human eyes."

"If you're being fresh with me," the big boy said,

"I'll beat you up. I'm nine, and you're not more than six."

"Seven," said the little one, who was just five.

"Well, even so, I'll beat you to a pulp."

"Go up to the wall, behind Emilio's grave. He's sitting there, the man the eyes belong to. You can ask him yourself whether it's true."

The big boy hesitated. The small one seized this opportunity to take his stick away and begin cautiously poking around on the bottom of the basin. He didn't want to hurt the eyes, they were surely very sensitive. The big one looked at him half in doubt, half in expectation.

"Well, where are they?" he asked after a while.

"They don't want to go home, that's the trouble," the little one said in dismay. "They're hiding."

"All lies."

"Then go up there and ask the man yourself."

"All right, I'll go and ask him. And if you've lied I'll beat you. In the meantime you can keep the stick."

"Good," said the small one.

He did not even look after the other, he was so busy. If only the water weren't so muddy! Blobs of fat swam in it. He poked and poked.

"Hey there, youngster," the women said to him. "Get away from here, stop being a nuisance."

They're not in the fountain, he thought, pulled the stick out of the water and ran up to the wall to make his report.

But the man without eyes had disappeared.

Oh, the small one thought in disappointment, now I've come too late. The eyes must have flown back while I was at the fountain, and the man couldn't wait for me any longer.

The big boy rushed at him furiously and shouted:
"Well, where is he, your eye man?"

"I don't know. He's gone away. He was sitting here,"
the small one answered sadly.

"And I'm supposed to believe that? Give me the
stick."

The little one gave it to him.

"And now I'm going to beat you."

The little boy did not try to run away. He raised his
arms to his face and waited for the blows.

The fog drifting over the wall grew thicker and
thicker. Phantoms moved on the graves. The colors of the
tin wreaths were veiled in mist. Sounds were muffled in
the fog. The bridal party blinked sleepily.

"Now we'll go to Grandfather," said the groom's
father. "We'll have our siesta there."

The crowd and its children and musicians got up.
Baskets creaked, dresses rustled, jugs bumped together
with hollow thuds. The mad girl started in terror from
her sleep.

"Yes, yes, we're coming," muttered the bridegroom's
father, striding ahead of the rest through the fog. "You
won't be neglected, Grandfather, we're already on the
way."

The procession straggled to the other side of the field
with the black crosses. Strangers were crouching on the
grandfather's grave. They belonged to the next grave, but
there was no more room there. As soon as they saw the
crowd gathering in front of the mound, they got up and
looked for another unvisited grave in the neighborhood.

The wedding guests lowered themselves onto Grandfather's mound, and those for whom there was no room lay on the path and between the graves, and behind Grandfather's grave was a mound that no longer had a cross; a few found places there.

"Whoever is lying in this grave certainly won't object to a few people sitting on him," said the bridegroom's father. "Just the opposite. Now it looks as though he also has a family among the living, who are visiting him on All Souls' Day."

The groom cushioned his bride's head on his lap and laid his own head in his mother's lap.

"Look," the aunt said to the bride's father. "He's finally coming to his senses. And it's about time. All he has left is this afternoon and tonight."

The musicians rolled themselves in their ponchos and began to snore. The two families pressed close together, and where it was warmest, the children snuggled in. Dogs sniffed at the wedding party; other visitors to the cemetery picked their way over them. They paid no attention, for they had given themselves up to sleep in honor of Grandfather in his grave.

Manuel had found a place for himself at the bottom of the cemetery, near the section that belonged to the rich. Here the little one would not find him so easily. He leaned against the wall and slept, and the bride's little sister, who had not let him out of her sight and had secretly slipped away from the procession to Grandfather's grave, crouched not far from him like a faithful dog. But he did not know that.

He saw a cloud of dark red butterflies whirling above

a river. The water reflected them, the whole landscape grew red beneath them. And then ten suns, a thousand suns, above a sulphur-yellow clearing. The clearing seemed familiar to him, the olive-colored bushes at its edge, withered grass. But he could not remember where he had seen it. How bright it was! He could not look at it for long, it blinded him.

The bridegroom was once again climbing the river bank in front of the white house. Curtains moved in the windows; eyes peered out. He was suddenly in the court-yard—he did not know how—ducked, crawled on all fours, expecting shots. Then a door squeaked. Were they coming? He was crouching in the courtyard in the full blaze of the sun, exposed to all eyes, wanted to spring up, scream, run, hurl himself head over heels out of this square courtyard, but he was stuck to the earth. Above him he saw a vulture circling, its wings were wider than the courtyard. He clung to the fountain, but the fountain exploded with a loud bang, and the bridegroom saw the vulture diving toward him and knew: now I am blind.

The bride's brother was sitting on a flower-covered hill. Monkeys tumbled in the flowers, whirling down the side of the hill, turning somersaults, bounding away into the valley.

Why have I a gun in my hand? he asked himself. What's it for? How do you make it fire? I can't remember.

He let himself fall into the flowers and laughed.

.   .   .

The bride's other brother had a woman in his arms. Her hat had fallen off, her eyelids were half closed. It was the woman he would never possess, for she was rich. Never had she given him a glance, never had he spoken to her, never had she heard his name. He had only seen her and that was enough. Now he held her in his arms, felt her body press against his.

Someone stepped on his hand. He leaped up and glared around. An old man had been climbing over him. But they lay so close together, how could anyone get by them without stepping on someone?

But the dream, the dream! Groaning, he let himself sink back again: that dream was over and gone.

The bridegroom's father was standing on a balcony, just the way the President had once stood on the balcony of the town hall in Marga-Marga. He was wearing a black suit with many orders on his breast; big, brightly colored crosses and stars. Behind him stood his son, his wife, his whole tribe. He leaned on the balustrade and looked down into the city square, which was black with the people of Marga-Marga and the neighboring towns.

Is this city really Marga-Marga? He examined the façades of the houses. Is it La Paz? The façades grew pale or hid themselves in shadow as soon as his glance fell on them. But the open square beneath him stayed bright, it glowed in the sun, dotted with lampposts, and on each hung a man. He himself had had them hanged, he, the President, lord over life and death. There hung the mine owner, the richest man in Marga-Marga. The President on the balcony laughed; wasn't the lamppost bending under the burden of that wealth?

From the next post dangled the lawyer; he had grown rich on the poor of Marga-Marga. The police chief hung there too, his uniform glittered in the sun, beside him the mayor. And in a long row hung the city fathers, behind them the merchants and all the military leaders of Bolivia. The man on the balcony had never seen them, so they all had the same face, the way he pictured a military leader to look. They were strung up along with the Paraguayan generals and you could not tell one from the other.

The Indios of Marga-Marga were wandering through the forest of lampposts with children and grandchildren; paused under some of the hanged men, stared up at them, half curious, half afraid, and whispered.

"Why are you whispering?" the bridegroom's father cried down. "Shout! Or are you afraid that your cries will bring them to life again? Lift up your children and shout! Where are the musicians? You must dance! Dance, you people! I will have more and more hanged, all the Spaniards, with Pizarro in the middle! Now the houses around the market place of Marga-Marga belong to us, ours the mines outside the town! Dance, you people, dance!"

The crowd among the lampposts began to move. Skirts whirled, flutes trilled. The somber colors grew bright, the plaza went wild, children screeched. The lampposts began to revolve, the hanged men turned with them, circled over the heads of the dancers, swinging wider and wider around the axes of the lampposts. The sun became blue, reddened in a black sky. Fireworks went up as on the President's birthday, feet stamped in the dance, the faces of the Indios glowed copper red.

To be free at last, to be rich, to be master! The

bridegroom's father with his whole tribe leaped from the balcony to join in the festival below.

I will lead him, thought the bride's small sister, who had stayed awake and was still huddling motionless beside the blind man. I will sing to him. I will tell him everything that goes on. He will miss nothing. I will raise flowers for him so that he can smell them. I will trickle wax from one of the consecrated candles on the altar of the Virgin of Copacabana into his eye sockets, then maybe his eyes will grow again. Maybe. Of course they will. Yes.

A red bird's head, tall as a tower, craned over the wall, bent down into the cemetery. The bride's father saw it and was terrified. But no one else seemed concerned about this monstrosity, whose beak sank lower and lower. The bird's eyes grew huge, glared down.

"Save yourselves!" cried the bride's father and dropped to the ground. The others laughed.

"The head!" he screamed.

"Where?"

The head had disappeared. The sky above the cemetery was clear. Now the bride's father was leaning over the cemetery wall and looking down at the graves. Cries arose. The people panicked, rushed away, they flattened themselves against the wall, threw themselves to the ground. He saw himself; his own face hung gigantic over the cemetery. Then everything was still. Even the grave wreaths stopped rattling. The drummer flung himself into the ditch beside Grandfather's grave, and didn't dare to breathe.

"All a joke!" laughed the tower-tall face above the

cemetery. Then it saw something red growing out of Grandfather's grave—a bird's head with jagged, crooked beak and hard eyes. It grew and swelled. It ruffled its feathers.

"Save yourselves!" cried the bride's father.

But the people were already rising from the ditches and from the graves, looking with relief at the sky and laughing: the face above the cemetery had disappeared. He himself, the bride's father, lay in Grandfather's grave under transparent earth, and a tin wreath rattled above him. Now the people were settling themselves on the mound again, passing around a brandy bottle.

"Give me some of that down here, you fellows, take pity!"

Where was the red bird's head? It was strutting in the fountain and snorting. It spattered the whole cemetery. Already the grass seed on the graves was growing green, shoots and vines shot upward, leaves unfolded. Buds opened. Flowers as big as a child's head, red as fire and yellow as the sun, a paradise garden. The tin wreaths grew fragrant.

"You people, come down to me," cried the bride's father, and pounded on the underside of the grave vault. "Come down and be merry!"

"Come up here instead," answered the wedding party. "The cemetery is blooming, do you still want to go on being dead down there? Everyone will arise! Come up and eat flowers with us!"

The bridegroom's mother brought a child into the world. It was a little boy, someone handed him to her. Thank God, a boy! But he had six fingers on each hand.

| 91

My husband will be angry at me. People in the streets will point at the little one. That must not be. I must bring a better child into the world!

Her body strained again in expectation: If only it is beautiful, if only it is without flaw!

Then she saw it lying there: a boy with a dog's head. She groaned aloud. Am I never to have a proper child?

She hid both of them in the goat pen. And once more she lay in the half darkness of the hut and labored. This time it was a beautiful, flawless child, only the size was wrong. The poor thing was as small as a newborn kitten. O sweet Virgin of Copacabana, misfortune lies upon me. Give me one single well-formed boy, so that my husband will be pleased with me. Grant me this before he comes home and gets angry!

The fog parted and drifted downhill. Afternoon sunlight flooded the cemetery. Groups moved wearily through the rows of graves, settled down anywhere and fell asleep. The dogs curled up. The wind died and the screeching of the tin wreaths with it. Only outside, beyond the cemetery, in the shadow of the wall, a disturbance arose. Women darted hastily around, carried jugs and cloths. Out there a child was being born.

Under a blooming bush in the garden of the missionary station deep in the Gran Chaco, cowered the bride's aunt in all her long-vanished beauty. She saw the vultures circling above her, and beside her lay the bridegroom. Was he dead?

His face was hidden in tall grass. She laid her hand on his breast. Was he breathing? Over in the courtyard they were singing. Was it day or night?

The bridegroom was breathing. She pressed herself against him. He stretched out his hand and felt for her, but his face was still hidden in the grass. He stroked her.

What did the vultures want? They circled lower.

"The vultures are coming," she whispered. "We must hide."

Already their wings were brushing the crests of the trees in the garden. In the courtyard the soldiers had stopped singing.

"We must flee!"

"Why flee?" whispered the bridegroom, and stroked her. "This has all happened already."

He turned his eyeless face toward her.

The guitar player had his arms around his instrument. He dreamed a dream that often plagued him.

She was standing upright in a niche of the inn on the Marga-Marga plaza. She flattened herself against the wall like a child playing hide-and-seek.

"Why, there you are, Mother," he gasped overjoyed, still breathless from running.

His mother put her finger to her lips. She was so young! Much younger than he; a young girl. Her face was the face of the Madonna of Copacabana. Did he dare to ask her the question, who his father was? She had never told anyone at all, but after all she must know, Lord God, who would, if not she? How beautiful she was! But, as always, she would not say.

"Why didn't you call me?" he asked. "Why didn't you wave to me?"

"Don't betray me," she whispered and smiled at him. "No one must know I am here."

He wanted to throw his arms around her for joy at having finally found her, wanted to carry her home in his arms. But he could not reach her. He stretched his hands out, but he could not touch her. She pressed herself still deeper into the niche, a little girl now, with anxious eyes.

"Don't play with the other boys," she whispered, and her lips twisted as though she were about to cry. "They have knives."

"Stay with me, then they won't hurt me," he answered softly.

She shook her head. "You'll betray everything," she said, and giggled.

"Come home with me," he begged.

She smiled. "Go home. I'll follow you. But you mustn't turn around. If you look back, I won't be there."

"I don't trust you. You have promised so often to come home, but then when I'm at home you're never there."

"You'll see."

He looked hard at her so that he could remember how she looked. She nodded to him, and then he believed her again and ran home through the empty streets. But when he opened the door and stared eagerly into the empty room, she was not there, and he knew that once more it had been a goodby. She had not followed him. She would not let herself be caught. That was how she was, he knew her well, although she had died when he was born. Where was her home, that restless one?

· · ·

The drummer was drifting in a river of colors—violet and yellow.

. . .

"What did you dream?" the bridegroom asked softly, lifted his head from his mother's lap and drew his bride toward him.

"About him," she whispered and pointed, smiling, to the sleeping drummer. "He was my bridegroom, not you."

The groom looked at the sleeper suspiciously. But he was still a youngster, fonder of playing with slingshots than going with girls. He still had very small hands and a child's face.

"I permit you to dream about him," said the bridegroom.

A child awoke and began to scream. It wakened other children. Their uproar amused the wedding party.

"All shit," said the guitar player.

"Why?" asked the bridegroom.

"That's how it is, all shit. You'll find out for yourself, if you're not too dumb. All to no purpose, you walk in place or walk in a circle, and in the end hell gobbles you up."

"He had a bad dream," said the bridegroom's mother.

"Have something to drink, then you'll feel better," called the older of the bride's brothers.

The drummer emerged from a cloud of lilac and yellow and a scent that emanated to him from the distinguished ladies of Marga-Marga; lifted his long eyelashes, drunk with sleep, and asked: "Where do we go now?"

"To my grandmother's grave," said the bride. "But it's still too early for dancing."

. . .

The bride's little sister sat lost in the contemplation of the sleeping face beside her, which glistened in the sun. Her eyes probed the scars, the sunken eyelids, the forehead, the veins at the temples.

Be quiet, all you in the cemetery, she thought. He's asleep. He must sleep for a long time, as long as he wants. He has earned it. It cost him great effort to get to the cemetery, and then the long story, and he must surely still be hungry. Let no one come and disturb him! I shall guard him.

She looked around angrily and kicked a dog that tried to sniff at him. Two girls wandered by and stopped in front of Manuel. They stared at him and giggled.

"How wide he opens his mouth," said one of them.

"How he snores," cried the other.

"Go away!" begged the little one.

"Why should we go away?" they asked. "We're not hurting you and we're not hurting him either. Have you by any chance rented the snorer? Or has he hired you as watchdog?"

They laughed loudly, and Manuel closed his mouth and moved in his sleep. Shadow fell over his sunken lids.

"You'll wake him up!" the little girl whispered reproachfully.

"Is he your brother?"

"No."

"Your cousin?"

"No."

"What is he to you then, that you're so concerned about him?"

"My fiancé."

"Dear God, when are you going to marry him? In ten years?"

"I'm already eleven."

If only he doesn't move, thought the little one. If only the shadow stays across his eyes. Otherwise they'll notice that he is blind, and laugh so loud it will wake him up.

"Now go on," she begged. "Now he has closed his mouth and isn't snoring any more. There's nothing more for you to see."

"And why isn't he in the Chaco?"

"He's already been down there and has come back."

"On leave?"

"For good. He is a hero. He is a general. He doesn't need to fight any more. They let him come home because he was such a good soldier."

"I've never heard of such a thing," one girl said. "My fiancé is down there too but he has not been sent home. Just the same, he is a good soldier, he has already killed lots of them. He had it put in a letter to us. He even ran his bayonet into one man's stomach."

"Not so loud, not so loud," the little one whispered anxiously.

"Then yours will probably come home soon too," said the other girl. "As soon as he becomes a general."

"But mine doesn't snore," said her friend. "And he is much handsomer than this one here."

They wandered on, and the bride's little sister sighed with relief, for Manuel had not awakened. He just sighed deeply a few times and let his head turn to the other side. Now all who came by could see that he was blind. She crouched in front of him.

V

THE WEDDING PARTY GOT UP SLEEPILY, STOOD AROUND Grandfather's grave and waited.

"Yes, it's still too early for dancing," said the bridegroom's father. "When the sun sets we'll meet at the bride's grandmother's. You know where her grave is. Then it will be your turn, you musicians. You have eaten and slept. You will have to play till you melt. And now everyone can go wherever he wants to."

The wedding party scattered. The bride's two brothers walked down the middle path toward the gate, for they knew that the fellows who had to go off into the Chaco tomorrow were standing together outside, grinning at one another, spitting now and then and discussing the Chaco. All were curious and anxious for the latest word, but none of them knew much. "We'll soon show them," they said.

The neighbors of the bride and bridegroom who were guests at the wedding went to visit graves of their own. Each had dead lying here, and none could be forgotten if one wanted to be safe from their vengeance. Women polished the tin wreaths with their skirts, men pressed the crosses that had been loosened by the wind deeper into the graves. The cemetery lay in sunlight, the crosses hung noiseless and motionless, for the wind had dropped. Gossip and laughter buzzed among the crosses.

The bridegroom's mother pulled the crazy girl to her feet.

"Come," she said, "now we're going to visit the children."

She crossed the middle path and entered the field of white crosses. The crazy one stumbled along behind her. In front of the grave of her eldest son the mother stopped. It was short and narrow and steeply mounded. The sun had long since faded the tin flowers, for the boy had only lived to be eight.

Jaime, do you hear me? the old woman thought. We are all together here in the cemetery.

The crazy girl watched her mother, who tumbled a little clay horse from out of her basket, heaped up the sand of the mound and planted it there.

He would have become a great man, the mother thought, a mayor or a priest. He learned to read without going to school. Why did I take him with me that time on the pilgrimage to Copacabana? It was just that he wanted to go so much, and it wasn't even the first time. He marveled again at Lake Titicaca and again he played with the shells on the shore. I bought him a little pennant for the procession. He crawled with me on his knees to the altar. That time I prayed for the little one and the crazy one, and he understood and helped me. But then on the way home the car ran over him. From one minute to the next he was dead. That's how we came back from the pilgrimage to Copacabana!

She bent low and whispered: "My Jaime, intercede for your big brother. He is going to the war."

Then she got up and went to the grave of her next child.

The little boy was going by with his family not far from the place where Manuel slept. He recognized him and stared: there was the man! He was astonished. Hadn't the eyes come back to him yet? Had they drowned somewhere in the fountain? Had someone stepped on them? But then he couldn't see anything!

He wanted to pull away from his mother's hand and run over to Manuel. But she held him firmly. He had to stay with her. But he kept turning around and looking at Manuel even though he stumbled over crosses and mounds, and had to be almost dragged along by his mother.

The bride's little sister, who was still crouching beside Manuel, stared after him angrily. This blind man belonged to her!

Now the bridegroom's mother was bending over another grave with white cross and faded wreath. Here lay Sergio, whom she had born after Jaime and the mad one. She had left him at home that time when she had gone on the pilgrimage with Jaime, for Sergio had always been sick. Despite the prayers in Copacabana, despite the intercession of his big brother, he had died.

What more was I to do? the mother thought. I nursed

him as long as I could, and carried him around longer than my other children.

She took a second clay horse out of the basket and placed it on the mound. The mad girl, who was crouching beside her, reached for it, but the mother slapped her hand.

Once I took him to the doctor's. The pills he prescribed didn't help either. And I had no money for a second visit. My Sergio, pray for your big brother. You will certainly be heard, for you never did anything wicked as long as you lived.

She said three Our Fathers, then she pushed the crazy girl in front of her to the grave of the youngest of her dead sons, which lay next to the wall and was tiny; the grave of a newborn infant.

Someone had stumbled over the cross and had knocked it down. She righted it. The wreath with its tin flowers was still bright. She pressed a third clay horse, baked a dark brown, into the earth at the foot of the cross.

Three days was all it had lived, and it was good, her husband said, that it died, for the child's right arm was withered. But she had wept hard when it died, just as though it had been a healthy child. She had hidden the little one from the people, no one had seen that arm, and only her husband and she knew about it. The mad girl had been there too, but she didn't tell because she couldn't talk.

Next year on All Souls' Day we'll come here again, Carlos, for a whole day. Goodby and don't forget what I have asked of you. He was married this morning. His bride is good. You can be sure that we chose wisely for him. And he is a handsome fellow—if only you could see him! Still young and timid, but he will grow, he will grow.

She recited a whole rosary, then took the crazy girl, who was pulling at the cross on a neighboring grave, by the hand and dragged her along, out of the field of white crosses, down the middle path and through the entrance of the cemetery, among the tables, booths, and carts.

"You want a jug? A little horse?"

"Wreaths, señora, wreaths!"

And a child's voice beside the gate: "Tortillas, tortillas!"

She did not look around, for now she was in a hurry. She trotted past the two police horses, past a row of donkey carts and a few wagons. From a big tent drifted the smell of beer. People were still streaming in from Marga-Marga, but others were already leaving the cemetery and turning homeward. The long road across the plain was dotted with figures.

The crazy girl clung to a cart on which toys were displayed. She pointed to the dolls and babbled.

"Don't be a fool," her mother said gently and pulled her away. "Where should I get the money?"

Behind a table she recognized the drummer. He was hawking lottery tickets with awkward gestures but great enthusiasm.

"What are you doing there?" she asked in surprise.

"I'm allowed to help here," he answered proudly. "Don Leo has gone into the cemetery for a while. He wants to visit his wife. Meanwhile I'm doing the selling, since Serafina has the day off. He explained everything to me. And I'll get three free chances when he comes back.

Every chance wins. I could win any of the things you see here. It's all really quite magnificent."

"Do you know the man?"

"He is from my village."

The crazy girl grabbed for a ball. The mother took it from her hand and put it back in its place.

"Don't forget," she said, "that by sunset you must be back inside with us. That's what you're paid for."

"Sure," the young man answered, and nodded. "The sun is still high. Don Leo is visiting his wife and then his uncle, but only for a short while. I'll be back with you before the sun turns red."

The old flute player was bored. He wandered through the rich people's section. Here at least there were a few real flowers, and on the graves stood columns and headstones and even weeping angels. He had no dead in this cemetery and it had always remained alien to him. He came from Santa Elena, a little town in the northern lowland of Bolivia, and for all the forty years he had lived up here he had been homesick. In the lowland the cemeteries were more beautiful, full of flowers, full of bushes and climbing vines, especially after the rainy season, and sometimes the cemetery of his village had even been under water when the river overflowed its banks. He thought of the church at the edge of that cemetery. Just a chapel, all white and full of pigeons. Since the village had been abandoned the little chapel had stood open and pigeons had nested there. He had been back home just once, on his way from Trinidad, and he had wanted to visit the cemetery too. That time the river was up to the chapel door; a lake overgrown with bushes and little trees whose roots hung in the water, a still body of water completely covered with *Victoria regia*. He had had to be taken out in an old rowboat, which parted the huge leaves that floated on the surface. The door of the chapel stood wide open, and when he went inside a flock of pigeons had risen and flown out over his head or winged through the empty window frames. They were nesting everywhere; in the pews, on the altar, in the choir gallery, even on the shoulders and laps of the holy statues. The floor of the chapel was coated white. The saints had disappeared under a white crust.

"Why don't you drive them away?" he asked the man who had rowed him from the village.

"We did," he answered.

"But they're still here!"

"They come back. And if it's not the same ones then it's others. They like the chapel."

"Then shoot them!"

"Can't do that. One of them might be the Holy Ghost."

After that he never went back to the lowland. The journey there took days. And how was he to get enough money together for that? And what should he do down there since his village was deserted? In Santa Elena frogs now croaked in the plaza. The primeval forest crept upon the empty houses and into them, darted its animal-like blossoms through the empty windows, through the doors, grew out of the roofs, forced its way through the pavement. Year after year it crept deeper into the town, until the bust of the general with the giant epaulets that stood in the plaza slowly disappeared beneath it. Gradually the shacks collapsed. The plague had left only a few survivors in Santa Elena, and those it had spared had moved to neighboring towns or to the big cities that lay higher up. It was over for Santa Elena.

When he became a soldier, chance had landed the flute player here in the highland and here he had stayed. But he hated this barren cemetery, this yellow clay in its quadrangle of walls, he hated the gray-yellow village and this whole bald, desolate highland.

They never have pigeons in this cemetery, he thought. That's how poor they are.

The rich people's cemetery was not crowded. A few ladies under black lace veils were bending over graves, decorated watering cans in their hands. They looked distrustfully at the flute player, who had sat down at the edge of an empty grave and was dangling his legs in the hole.

I shouldn't have listened to Manuel when he was talking about the lowland, he thought. Now he has stirred it all up again.

On the bottom of the freshly dug grave lay a woman's hat. The wind had driven it into a corner where the shadows fell.

Why should I take the trouble to get it out? he thought. I have no wife. Besides, it probably isn't even new.

"Are you a gravedigger?" asked a lady who was passing the open grave but had shrunk back a step, because he stank.

"No, señora, I am a musician."

"What are you doing here?"

"Nothing."

"This grave is for Señorita Marisol."

| 105

He nodded. Yes, he knew Señorita Marisol, and he had also heard that she was dying. Sometimes he had seen her slowly crossing the plaza in Marga-Marga, a fat old lady with stiff back and swollen face. Her clothes were very elegant, for she had spent most of her life in the city.

"I think," the lady went on, "that her relations would not be pleased to find someone sitting on the edge of her grave and dangling his legs, someone who doesn't belong here at all. You do know that the police chief of Marga-Marga, Don Eugenio, is her nephew? He has also come out here today and must be somewhere about. I advise you to move over to your own cemetery."

She disappeared among the graves and watched him from a distance. He got up slowly, buried his hands in his trouser pockets, tucked the flute under his arm, spat in a high arc into the grave, and strolled off whistling.

When the mother turned the outer corner of the wall, leaving the tents and booths behind and starting up the slope, she came upon the altars to the dead. Here, sheltered by the wall, all along it to the highest corner, under little canvas tents which would not have reached even to the shoulder of the bride's small sister, stood the food prepared for the dead. Meat and bread on tin plates and new wine in clay jugs stood ready, heaped in pyramids and flanked by candles.

The mother walked back and forth, comparing and rejecting, until she had finally found a spot that seemed suitable for the altar to her own dead. She let go of the crazy one, set the heavy basket on the ground and out of it drew an old tarpaulin. The wind caught in the folds of the cloth, filled it and tore it from her hands. With endless patience she made it into a little tent, securing the upper corner in a hole in the wall. She drew the two lower edges straight out from the wall and held them down with stones. Now the wind could not disturb the altar she was going to build under the tent.

She began to gather clumps of clay. The mad girl watched her attentively and understood. She too began eagerly collecting stones and clods until she found two white pebbles and struck them together. Sparks leaped! She squatted down and buried herself in this game, and her mother didn't bother her, but let her go on playing undisturbed. She built up the rubble under the tent into a step pyramid. Over it she spread a woolen cloth, which she had woven herself, and placed two candles on it.

"You needn't feel ashamed in front of the others," she said to her dead and examined the altars nearby. "Your altar is as fine as any."

On the top of the pyramid she placed a tin cross. Then from her basket she unpacked plates of meat and bowls with cake and bread: meat which she had saved for months to buy and which her family could afford only on holidays; a cake she had baked the day before with beating heart; would it satisfy the dead? She had bought the ingredients, brand new, special, and very expensive. To pay for them she had had to sell a lot of sheep's cheese in the market. This was no tortilla, but a cake made of genuine wheat. None of the wedding guests had been allowed to taste it, the best of the All Souls' banquet had been kept for the dead, for they, the three dead brothers of the recruit, should be well disposed toward the last son that remained to her. On the top step of the altar, under the cross, she laid three pieces of licorice for the three little ones. They would certainly like something sweet.

The guitar player had joined the fathers of the bridal pair, who were standing in a circle of men bargaining beside the fountain. One was talking about a sheep he wanted to sell, the other was handing around a pair of spectacles. His daughter, the bride's little sister, had found them a few weeks before, distinguished-looking spectacles, lying in the middle of the plaza. Now he wanted to sell them, for he needed money. He was the bride's father, he had had to go into debt. The spectacles passed from hand to hand. He was willing to sell them cheap.

The men held them to their eyes and laughed. A remarkable instrument. It made everything blurry. What lawyers and directors and all the rich people were willing to put up with to look rich!

"Offer them to those down there, they have money," said an old man. "They can afford glasses. There goes the police captain. Maybe he wants them!"

The guitar player was allowed to look through them too, but he saw only mist. You could take the glass out, he thought, then you could see better. But I can't pay for them, either with or without glass.

He handed the spectacles on and left the group of men. Up there on the slope was his mother's grave, and he hadn't visited her yet. He had time now. He walked up through the rows of graves to her, settled himself cross-legged on her mound and began to smoke. He had only a single cigarette, which he smoked slowly and solemnly until only a tiny butt was left. But he had time. The sun would not touch the horizon for quite a while. He strummed on his guitar, and out of the strumming came a song. At first he sang it softly, then louder and louder. The people on the neighboring graves grinned, for it was a child's song:

> *There rode a nun*
> *on a nanny goat*
> *way back, way back*
> *on the goat her bum,*
> *with a veil so white.*
> *Tin, tin, tan, tan,*
> *O Santa Maria,*
> *with a veil so white . . .*

The flute player came wandering through the graves and could hear him from far away. During the second stanza he crept up close behind the singer's back.

> *Oh whither away*
> *through the heat of the day?*
> *To sprinkle the flowers*
> *gold, silver and white,*
> *the flowers in heaven,*
> *Tin, tin, tan, tan,*
> *O Santa Maria,*
> *the flowers of heaven . . .*

"So you sit there," the flute player said. "You sit there all alone and sing. May I join you?"

"Sit down," called the guitar player. He stopped singing and placed his guitar beside the grave. "My mother had only one son and in other respects she was, so to say, alone. And so there's plenty of room. It will be an honor for her."

"Damn highland, damn dog's life up here," said the old man, and sat down. "I don't ever want to be buried here."

"You won't have any choice, or do you think they'll ship your carcass down special, and free of charge besides?"

"When I see it's coming to that, then I'll simply walk away, then I'll get myself down there, as far as I can. In any case I want something growing on top of me."

"Then get going, or it'll be too late. You already stink of old age. Sooner or later you'll fall apart."

"Don't fool yourself," the flute player replied angrily. "It's just the highland that gives me trouble. If I were down there then I'd show you, I know my way around there, I'm at home there. Nothing like that would have happened to me!"

"What?"

"What happened to Manuel. Nobody wants to go down into the lowland, but they're forced to whether they want to or not. And I, I want to, but they won't take me!"

"I tell you you're too old!"

"If they'd only take me down there I wouldn't care what they did with me after that. They could impale me or cut me in quarters for all I care. Just to be there! I was in Marga-Marga and tried to volunteer, but they laughed at me. There's no old-age home there, they said. But at least I could ladle out soup and chase the snakes away. And even if they blinded me for it, I'd do it!"

He took out a deck of cards. "She won't object, will she?" he asked, pointing downward as he shuffled.

"Deal for three. She can play too. I'll hold her hand for her."

"But then you'll have an advantage."

"Why don't you cut your mother in too?" asked the guitar player. "She could play, couldn't she?"

"But she's buried in the lowland."

The guitar player thought for a while, then he pointed to the next grave and said: "That dead man there has no visitors. Shall we have him join us?"

The flute player nodded, and so they played four-handed.

The flames on the altar guttered, but the little tent kept them from going out. The mother got up.

"Come here and look," she called to the mad girl. She was still sitting spread-legged on the ground and striking sparks from the stones.

The mother laughed softly, swept a clear place in front of the altar with her hand, knelt down and became absorbed in telling her beads. The wall was already throwing long shadows across the plain. The landscape had a lilac-blue tinge, flickering orange lights along the hillside and plowing furrows of turquoise into the mountains. Birds circled over the cemetery. The crazy girl suddenly threw her stones away and stared up. The game was over.

The bridal pair wandered in silence along the inside of the wall. They did not know what to talk about. From time to time they cleared their throats and threw stolen glances at each other. They had already talked about the Chaco, and nothing else came to them. The bridegroom crossed over to the middle path, for he felt drawn to the square outside, to the tents and the booths, and his bride followed him, keeping a pace behind; she knew what was expected of a married woman.

"There's Manuel sitting over there," he said. "He's asleep. And your little sister is sitting beside him. She's watching over him—look!"

"She's gone to sleep," said the bride. "I don't know what she sees in Manuel. He's so proud he's almost bursting. At the same time he looks like a ghost. He treated you as though you didn't know anything about the Chaco. Only what he says is supposed to be right. But what is he compared to you? You have eyes. He has none. He should behave with modesty instead of talking big. And besides, I hate him. Do you know what the people say? The baby the little kitchen helper at the Atahualpa had is his!"

"Well, what of it?" said the bridegroom. "He has lost his eyes. That's atonement enough for a lot of things. I feel sorry for him and I would like you to feel sorry too."

"But I hate him!"

He stopped and threw her an angry glance. She lowered her head.

"Listen to me," he said. "My father won't stand any talking back. I don't want him to beat you. And so do what he says and agree with him."

She was silent and trotted after him once more, an obedient bride.

"Señorita Marisol is on her deathbed," he said as they passed through the field of the rich, happy to have found a subject of conversation.

"Yes," she answered from behind him.

112

She was trying to match steps with him, but she was much shorter than he. She kept getting out of step.

"Do you know her?"

"Yes. She is very distinguished, but I can't stand her. She can't stand us either."

"Didn't your aunt work for her?"

"Only for barely a year, when Señorita Marisol and Don Eugenio came with his mother from the city. Before my aunt there had already been two maids, but Señorita Marisol couldn't get on with either one; after a couple of days they both were fired. My aunt lasted longer. She knows how to get along with fine folk, you know. She hears everything that happens in the town and tells her employers. They like that. But it wasn't easy with Señorita Marisol; nothing suited her. She kept moaning for the city, she cursed Marga-Marga. She supposedly called it a filthy hole. She even said it stinks of poor people. My aunt heard her."

"Then why did she come here?"

"What else could she do? They lost their house in the city, and then Don Eugenio let himself be transferred here. She has no one but him, her nephew, for his mother is already very old and childish, my aunt said. Señorita Marisol had to come with him to Marga-Marga whether she wanted to or not. She had no husband, of course, and so she couldn't stay alone in the city."

"And now she is dying even sooner than his mother."

"She was too fat. She hardly ever moved, my aunt said, she always sat in an easy chair, and while she sat there she either dreamed with open eyes or talked about the city. That's why she had the stroke, that's certain."

"It will be a big funeral. After all, she's Don Eugenio's aunt."

"My aunt said that even she would go, even though Señorita Marisol drove her out that time. And why? Just because she took a blouse, which was too small for Señorita Marisol anyway. And besides, more, she had so many blouses she didn't know them all. Before Don Eugenio's brother died, they were very rich. He kept track of everything, my aunt said, and she understands those things. Don Eugenio is a good-hearted man, she says, but he doesn't know anything about money. Whatever he earns he drinks, and that's also the reason they transferred him here, she says."

He had never heard her talk so much. He stopped and turned around. Then she was embarrassed and silent. They both stared at the ground in silence.

"She has already had extreme unction," the bride stammered after a while.

"Are you going with them to the funeral?" he asked.

"Of course. Everyone will go."

"Yes."

"And you?"

"I? You know I must leave tomorrow morning."

"Oh yes."

They were silent once more.

"When you come back, I'll tell you all about it," the bride finally said. "An expensive funeral with a white coffin, they say. Of course she has always remained a virgin."

"Why didn't she die yesterday?" the bridegroom asked and walked on a way. "Then she could have been buried today, on All Souls' Day. She couldn't have found a better day, all of Marga-Marga is in the cemetery, and the other villages too. They would all have looked on."

"Her heart is still very strong, my aunt said, it might take a couple of days more. But she doesn't recognize anyone now. As God wills, she said."

"So be it," the bridegroom answered.

"Yes," said the bride, and now she had nothing more to tell him, for everything about Señorita Marisol had been said.

They left the cemetery and joined the crowd around the booths. The bridegroom discovered the drummer and grinned at him.

"Three chances for twenty!" the young man cried, red with excitement.

The bridegroom turned around.

"Do you want three chances or would you rather have licorice?" he asked the bride.

"Licorice," she said and looked at him with admiration. How good he was. Here he was buying her licorice. She gave half of it to him.

"Licorice was always my favorite," she said.

"That's strange," he replied. "Mine too. We belong together. Yes, really, isn't that odd? We both like licorice best. I will bring you licorice from Paraguay."

She smiled and nodded gratefully while the licorice string hung from her mouth and grew shorter bit by bit.

"The people call me 'señora' now," she said. "Have you heard them? Now I am a señora. And yet I am just sixteen."

"You will live with my parents. You will help my mother. You will have a bed next to my sister, behind the partition, until I come back."

"Next to your sister?" the bride cried in dismay. "I'm afraid of her. She's so crazy, she can't even talk!"

"She will get used to you, and you will get used to her. She can be very sweet. I like her."

"She terrifies me," cried the bride. "I can't stand her with her stupid eyes! When I was doing washing for Don Delicio's wife she came along to the stream, and do you know what she did? She spread grass in the water, and then she took the soap away from me and licked it, and then she made a face and spit and threw the soap in the stream. I couldn't get it out again. Don Delicio's wife took that out of my pay. And when I slapped your sister's hand for doing it, she pulled my hair. She's so crazy! I wish you didn't have a sister. What shall I do if she pulls my hair again? I'll pinch her arm!"

"You must stay calm," said the bridegroom.

"Why don't you marry her off? Then she'd be out of the way."

"Who would have her? She can't even talk, she can't do anything!"

"But she could have children. Ask Manuel. He is blind, he won't get a wife the way he is. Give him your sister, then he'll have one."

"Be quiet," said the bridegroom. "You don't understand anything about it."

He attached himself to the group of fellows who were talking about the Chaco, and she took up her position behind him and waited patiently.

VI

AFTER THE MOTHER HAD COMMENDED HER LAST SON TO the Madonna and all the saints, she got up from the altar to the dead and shook the dust out of her skirts. Now there was only one thing more she had to do: visit the ancient Louisa.

She took the crazy one by the hand and they climbed up the hillside to a far corner of the cemetery. There she emerged from the shadows into the light of the sun, which was already very low and slowly growing red. It blinded her so that she had to close her eyes. When she opened them again, she saw a young woman lying on the ground under a poncho. Her hair clung to her sweat-streaked face. Two women crouched close by and whispered to her. On the lap of one of them lay a newborn child. It was wrapped in a cloth, the tiny face almost disappearing in the folds. Vessels with dirty water stood around. The other woman threw lumps of clay at the dogs that were lurking nearby.

The mother nodded to the woman in childbed. She knew her. Her husband was in the Chaco.

Louisa sat clad in black and full of dignity in her accustomed place under a tent behind the upper wall of the cemetery, and was even fatter than the year before. Around the entrance to the tent people squatted and waited to be called. The mother crouched beside them and drew the mad girl to her. This was not her first visit. She knew she would have to wait.

The aged Louisa came from the neighboring town. Every year on All Souls' Day she would set up her tent here and hold consultations. She was not cheap, but anyone without money could pay for her services with a rooster or a cheese, with eggs or cloth. On this she was open to reason, and for that the people were grateful to her.

Her daughter, a small, dried-up person, already well along in years, bustled about and took in the payments. In the back of the tent, hidden behind a curtain, chickens with tied legs lay cackling. It smelled of cheese. Now and then the old lady would burst out in anger at her daughter. Then she would toss her head like a frightened chicken and cower, and those waiting would cower with her. It was dangerous to make the aged Louisa angry. She had great power, she could be vengeful. One had to keep on good terms with her.

True, she had not been able to cure the mad girl even for a rooster, but when all three sons had died and the mother had seemed much too old for childbearing, Louisa had nevertheless helped her to a fourth son, the bridegroom. Today the mother planned to ask her to make this last son invulnerable.

"Have you come about your son?" Louisa asked, when the mother's turn came.

"Yes."

"He must also go down into the Chaco tomorrow?"

"Yes."

"A difficult matter. How much can you pay?"

"The harvest was bad, and I have to give my boy something to take with him . . ."

"Magic that costs nothing doesn't work."

"How much must I pay so that he will stay alive?"

"Two dozen eggs."

"But I have only one dozen, and a cheese. Will you do it for that?"

"Hand them over. And now your Heart of Jesus medallion."

The mother detached it from her neck and handed it to the old woman. With open mouth she watched as Louisa, murmuring spells, dipped it in a clay jug. The crazy girl pulled at her mother, babbling and pointing at a child who could barely hold up her huge hydrocephalic head. But the mother ignored her. She was completely absorbed in the magic that was happening. People said there was blood in the jug. Blood against blood, therein lay the magic. Louisa pulled the medallion on its chain out of the jug. Dark drops clung to it, round as berries. She held it over a candle and murmured even more softly than before. The mother listened in awe. Now Louisa swung the medallion over her head, eleven times, twelve times, the chain whistled in the air. Then she handed it to the mother and said: "Put this around your son's neck, but tell him positively that he must never take it off, otherwise the magic is gone."

People were already pushing into the tent from behind. The mother got up, drew the crazy girl up with her, and bowed almost to the ground in front of Louisa. Secure in the assurance that now nothing could happen to her son, she went away.

I have done everything for him that I can do for him, she thought. He is protected in many ways. He will not fall. He will come back and give his wife children. He will make me happy in my old age with all his sons and daughters.

She closed her hand tight around the medallion so as not to lose it. He must never take it off. Nor would he, if she begged him not to. He was an obedient son.

She heard the crazy girl jabbering behind her and stopped.

"Just come along," she said quietly. "I'm not running away from you."

In the tent in front of the cemetery gate Don Eugenio was sitting with Don Ramón, the owner of the Hotel Atahualpa. The police chief was not in uniform, he was drinking a glass of beer and nodding occasionally to those who passed the entrance to the tent or came inside.

That's the penalty he has to pay for being police chief, people thought. He must let himself be seen. Today is All Souls' Day. Every police chief comes to the cemetery on All Souls' Day, even if for only an hour. Here Don Eugenio's aunt is dying at home, but he has to be here, the poor fellow.

They looked at him sympathetically and greeted him with deep bows.

"Manuel is in the cemetery," said Don Ramón.

"Which Manuel?" asked Don Eugenio. "There are as

many Manuels as there are grains of sand on the seashore."

"My waiter. Don't you remember him? The one whose eyes they shot out."

"Oh, him."

"I hadn't seen him since he got back. He's in horrible shape, the poor wretch."

"He'll get a pension."

"You know yourself what those pensions amount to. If he doesn't do some begging as well he's probably done for. And what a picture of a man! It wasn't just the employees who were crazy about him, but the guests also treasured him, especially the women, who would turn around and look at him; in fact sometimes they called him to their rooms. Once in a while I had to check it a bit, but he was a good waiter, caught on fast. He was clean and smart at figures. When I had to travel, I left the management to old Gonzales. But actually it was Manuel who looked after everything. And now this!"

"War is war," said Don Eugenio.

"I sent word to him that he could come back to me, in the kitchen. There's all sorts of work there that a blind man could learn to do. But he didn't want to. He simply refused. I can understand. Now he's at the parish house. But that won't last long. He's too rebellious. Say, why don't you take him into your house?"

"I?" asked Don Eugenio in dismay and raised his eyebrows. "Why just me?"

"You earn well, and you have a garden. He could work it."

"No, no," Don Eugenio cried hastily, "that won't do, my aunt is against it."

"But—begging your pardon—you know she can't last much longer."

"Yes, yes, but even after her death I don't want to do anything against her wishes, I owe her that, and besides, we have no room for him, and who knows whether he would get on with the other servants? No, that won't do. You have absurd notions, Ramón."

"Well, all right," Ramón said. "It was only a question. I simply feel sorry for him. Imagine what it would be like if your eyes were suddenly shot out."

"Mine?" said Don Eugenio and goggled at Don Ramón. "Where did you get that idea? I'm not in the Chaco."

"Perhaps you will still have to go down—if things get worse?"

"Not I," said Don Eugenio, and leaned back. "I know the people in authority in La Paz. That's what counts."

"True enough," murmured Don Ramón.

"I like this holiday," said Don Eugenio, becoming animated. "It's gay and sad at the same time, a piquant festival. You literally see the dead taking part."

"You've been here in the cemetery all afternoon. Don't you have to go home? Your aunt is dying."

"The hell with that," replied Don Eugenio. "You're my friend, this is something I can say to you: I'm sick and tired of her dying. She's been dying for a week already. No man can stand that. Now she can only get one eye open. The other is paralyzed. When I'm sitting there beside her, suddenly that eye pops open and stares at me and stares after me if I get up and start to go away. Her body lies there as though dead, only her eye moves. I tell you again: no man can stand that. A bit of luck that today is All Souls' Day, a few hours vacation from her. Besides, the house is full of people. She is well looked after."

"Every time I came to see you, she was sitting there in her chair and gabbling about the life in the city. I admired you for being able to stand that incessant chatter."

"No," said Don Eugenio, "she didn't chatter all the time. Sometimes she would become very silent, when we were alone, especially during the early afternoon. Then she sat in her chair and smiled. I don't believe you ever saw her really smile. I always looked away. She could make your blood run cold with her smiles."

"Poor girl," said Don Ramón, and grinned. "She probably was never in love, eh?"

Both broke into laughter and clinked glasses.

"To love!"

They got up and left the tent.

"I'm going to ride home," said Don Ramón. "I've been here and people have had a chance to see me. Now I'm going home. Will you come along?"

"I'll stay a bit longer. The candles will burn well today, the wind has dropped. I like to watch the lights."

"God," said Don Ramón, and shrugged his shoulders, "the same thing every year."

"What's more, I don't want any killings this time. Last year there were two and the year before, one. You know how people lose their heads as soon as it gets dark."

"Can you prevent it?"

Don Eugenio laughed.

"Well then, adiós," said Don Ramón. "Don't stay too long. The people will begin to wonder. Think of your aunt's smile."

"She'll have the laugh on all of you," replied Don

Eugenio. "If she dies this evening she will dance all night over the roofs of Marga-Marga with the lover she never had."

"God protect us," cried Don Ramón. "She will crush us!"

"Hello," said the two card players on the grave, "there you are at last. What have you been up to all this time?"

The drummer laid his drum next to the grave and sat down with them. "I've been helping Don Leo in the lottery booth. I won too. He let me draw three times, free, for helping him. This is my lucky day."

He dug in his trouser pocket and brought out a big glittering button.

"This I'm going to give to my mother. She can wear it on the front of her blouse. Have you ever seen such a button?"

The old man spat, took the button in his hand, examined it from all sides and nodded. "A fine piece, a fine piece."

"And the second?" asked the guitar player.

"The second was a caramel candy. I've already eaten that because it was getting soft. But the third, that's the best."

Out of another pocket he pulled a tiny mirror.

"Just look in this, both of you—you have my permission, for as long as you like. It's an especially good mirror for shaving, Don Leo said. That's lucky, for it won't be long before I begin."

He stretched out his chin so that the two could judge.

"I've had a chance to look in other mirrors too," the

boy said. "But this way, in a mirror of one's own, one looks quite different."

"You're a handsome fellow," said the guitar player.

"I think so too," said the drummer. He beamed all over his thin pockmarked face.

"The sun is going down," said the old man. "It's time."

They got up, took their instruments and strolled over to the grandmother's grave. Sun still lay on the hill and threw long diagonal shadows across the cemetery. The colors of the tin wreaths were changing: the black crosses glowed dark red, the white were like rosy flames.

Manuel awoke. He sensed that it was evening, for the air had grown cooler and the voices in the cemetery had a hollow ring. He stood up and felt his way past the bride's small sister, who lay rolled up near him and did not notice him leaving. He wanted to run, after that long sleep. Now he was awake, now he must do something.

"It will be dark soon," someone near him said. "Then the dancing will begin."

I'll go out when they start dancing, he thought. I can't stand here and listen without dancing myself. I've always taken part as long as I've been in Marga-Marga. Everywhere they would call to me: Dance with us, Manuel, you put zing into people! No, I'll have to go outside so that I'll have the wall between me and them.

He groped his way through the entrance and between the booths and tents toward the east wall of the cemetery, now throwing long shadows across the plain.

"Are you going home already, Manuel?" someone asked.

"No, I'm just taking a walk around the cemetery. It's such a fine evening."

"Don't fall over the altars to the dead."

"I'll fall over whatever I feel like."

He made a wide circle, for the beer tent was in the corner, and came to the wall again, which led uphill. Here stood all the altars to the dead; he touched their awnings, the cloths, stumbled over a bowl probably rolled out by the wind. There was no one here now, he could hear that. It was still here, the people had withdrawn into the cemetery before dark. He raised his arms and let them fall again, he had had his sleep. Now he was awake, he had to do something.

Could I still manage a handstand? he thought.

He succeeded, and he took a few steps on his hands. But he became entangled in his poncho which trailed on the ground.

Weren't those soft footsteps he heard behind him? Didn't he hear the rustling of clothes? Someone was sitting down. And he had thought that he was all alone here. He got to his feet again and listened.

"Who's there?" he asked angrily.

"It's me, Serafina."

"Serafina? You? What are you doing here?"

"I'm simply sitting here and doing nothing."

"Why did you creep up on me?"

"I creep up on you?"

"You've just come. I heard your footsteps."

"You must be mistaken. I've been sitting here for ages. It's so peaceful out here."

He heard from which direction her voice came, and turned toward it.

"Here, between the two altars," she said. "More to the left."

"Talk, then I can follow your voice."

"Sit next to me."

She lifted her hand to him and drew him down.

"You should be inside," he said. "They'll be starting to dance any minute."

He huddled near her and leaned against the wall.

"I'm a widow," she replied. "I'm not allowed to dance. It has been hardly a year."

"You used to dance well. I saw you sometimes."

"You danced well too."

"Yes, that I did."

"It's already dark here," she said after a while, "but on the other side of the wall it's still light."

"It doesn't matter to me on which side I sit."

"But it's colder here."

"Are you chilly?"

She didn't answer, but he heard her poncho rustling.

"Do you still remember the night I took you home?" he asked, feeling for her arm.

"Be still—"

"It was even colder than tonight. Hoarfrost lay on the poncho we covered ourselves with. When we got up, it was quite heavy with frost, I had to shake it off. And there even was frost in your hair. But we weren't cold."

"No, we weren't cold."

"Only our fingers, later, when we tried to tie your hairnet again."

"Oh yes, my hairnet. It's still torn. I have it at home."

Now he had his hand under her poncho and was feeling his way up her arm. Her breasts had become even fuller than before; her blouse stretched over them.

"Oh no," she sighed, but she leaned against him and let his hand do what it wanted. With a languid motion she stroked his hair. He had beautiful, full hair.

"Serafina!" he cried.

"For God's sake," she whispered in panic, "the people can hear us. O Madonna!"

He pulled her to him.

"How can one resist you?" she sighed. "You're so strong. You do it so well. Just the way you used to."

"Yes," he cried, "yes, I am just as I used to be!"

"Talk softly, people can hear you all the way inside the cemetery. Think what would happen if somebody came by!"

"It's already completely dark here by the wall between the altars. So dark that you can no longer see anything either. Here we are equal. Oh, Serafina, come!"

"I'm right here. Yes, I want it."

He threw himself over her and pressed her against the earth.

"Watch out, the altar," she moaned. "You're pushing me against the altar. You probably haven't had a woman since it happened, have you?"

"Since what happened?"

"Oh you know, the thing with your eyes."

"Be still!"

"Watch out for the altar—"

He did not hear, he did not want to hear, he tore her blouse open so violently that the buttons flew off, and burrowed his face in her clothes. He did not notice that the altar which Serafina's head was leaning against was collapsing. A dish clattered, a jug fell down. Wine ran into the clay. It was a poor sort of altar, it wasn't even covered with canvas, but protected by only a thin cloth, an old sheet folded three times. Two candles fell over, a third remained upright. Now no longer sheltered by the windscreen, it gave off a modest light. Serafina sensed it through her closed eyelids.

"Put out the light," she groaned.

But he heard nothing now, he was possessed. She felt him trembling. He pulled at her skirts. She helped him. Suddenly her eyes flew open. What was that bright light? She twisted around in alarm. The sheet had caught fire. The flames were leaping up.

"Manuel!" she screamed.

"Yes," he gasped, "yes, yes."

"There's a fire behind me!"

He lifted his face from her breast, a distorted face without eyes, illuminated by the glow of the fire.

"No!" she screamed. "No, not with you, not with you! I can't!"

She pushed at him, while he stared at her in confusion with his eyeless sockets; shoved him away, sprang up and threw her poncho around her.

"What's the matter?" he asked. "Why do you suddenly not want to? Did I hurt you? I didn't mean to."

"I can't any more," she replied and started to cry. She held her blouse closed with both hands, although he could not see her. He stood up and groped for her.

"Be careful, you're walking into the fire," she said.

"Where are you?"

"I'm going now. Don't hold it against me, Manuel, but I can't."

He stood before her and let his hands fall.

"Why did you want to before, but not now?" he asked.

She trembled. "You frightened me so terribly."

"I frightened you? But we were both wild for it!"

"That's not it."

"What then?"

"Oh, leave me alone."

"What was it? You must tell me. I must know!" Manuel cried.

"I don't want to hurt you," she sobbed. "I didn't want to, but it came over me, it got hold of me like pincers!"

"Was it my face?"

She wept aloud and ran away. She was so distraught that she ran in the wrong direction—uphill. He stood listening after her and did not stir.

The burning sheet died down. It was dark again. Dogs busied themselves with the overturned plates. After a while Manuel felt his way to the wall and sank down against it. There was a smell of ashes.

On the other side of the cemetery mother and daughter were wandering downhill again. The mother carried her medallion like a treasure. Now and then she opened her hand and looked at it. It had been a wedding present from her husband, and now her son would wear it, day and night, and nothing would happen to him.

On this side of the cemetery, which was exposed to the wind and the evening glow, there were also a few altars to the dead. A woman crouching in front of one of them grinned at the bridegroom's mother with a snaggle-toothed grin.

"Were you up there too?"

"Yes."

The mother's eyes began to flicker, she knew this woman, she knew that her son had been killed. She took hold of the crazy girl and tried to run away, but the woman laughed.

"Why are you running away?" she asked.

The mother didn't answer.

"As you can imagine, I was also up there before he had to leave. She even dipped my medallion twice. She did double magic that was supposed to be completely certain. I even gave her a whole chicken. And in spite of that he fell."

"He must have taken the medallion off in the Chaco," cried the bridegroom's mother anxiously.

"They found him with the medallion around his neck!" shouted the mother of the fallen man.

The crazy girl stopped and looked behind her.

"Don't pay any attention to her!" cried the mother and pulled her on. "She lies!"

"I lie!" laughed the woman by the wall. "Of course I lie. My son has not fallen. He is in fine spirits and writes me every day. And I never went to see Louisa, I made it all up in my imagination. Is that what you'd prefer?"

The mother didn't answer. She did not want to hear, but she did hear. Each single word pressed shrill in her ears.

"Why should my son die and not yours?" the woman cried and ran after her. "Why should I be worse off than you? Why should I be alone and not you? He was a good boy, and I was no worse than you. All must fall, all!"

"Not mine," gasped the mother.

"All, all!"

"Don't listen to her," the mother cried at the mad girl. "None of it's true. Pablo is safe!"

She fled into the market throng in front of the cemetery, past the carts and booths, and dragged the crazy girl back through the gate.

Loud music swelled toward her. Three groups of musicians had begun to play in different parts of the cemetery and had attracted a crowd of people. One group was camped beside the fountain, another at the crossing of the central walk, a third beside the upper wall. In the confusion of different melodies the mother at once distinguished the music of the wedding party. The drummer was so good that, old though she was, her feet began to tingle. People would envy the bridal pair on account of this drummer.

She strode up the central walk. Now that she had done everything she could for her son, she felt empty and useless. The medallion in her hand had grown warm. What if it did not help? But it would, it would help, it had been in Louisa's jug, it had to help, and also Louisa had helped her to this son, everything was all right and in order, and nothing would happen to him, he would have no accidents, the bullets would whistle over him and spare him.

On the upper part of the slope lay the grave of the bride's grandmother, at the edge of the walk that ran along the wall. Here there was enough space, here the three musicians had set themselves up on the mound and were playing. The bridal pair danced among other couples. Skirts unfolded like peacocks' tails. The earth trembled under the leaping.

Now we're all here, thought the mother. The whole family is together again and all my four sons.

She took a short cut and walked across the field of crosses. The crazy girl trotted behind her.

"Where have you been?" the bridegroom asked, as his mother joined the circle.

"Just go on dancing," she said.

VII

THE MUSICIANS WERE SWEATING. THE GUITARIST HAD TO sing at the top of his lungs, for the evening air swallowed up the notes of his song. More and more dancers joined the group. They overflowed the path. They danced on Grandmother's grave and on others nearby. The grandmother wouldn't mind that, she would consider it a great honor that so many had come to her grave.

"Beat your drum, lad!" cried the bride's father. "No more tests now. I have paid you."

It was growing dark—time to light the candles on the graves. The best part of the fiesta had begun.

The bride's little sister was cold. She woke up and looked for Manuel, but he was gone. She sprang to her feet and stared around, she ran through the rows of crosses and along the inside of the wall, she even crept past that eerie corner of the upper cemetery where the woman who had killed herself was buried. But he wasn't there. She ran down the broad central path and searched in the rich people's cemetery. From far off she heard the first sounds of the music.

That's them, she thought. Now they're all together. I must go too, so they can see me, otherwise they'll be looking for me. Just for a quarter of an hour, that should be long enough.

She slipped through the graves and joined the wedding party. The guitar player was singing. His voice rang through the whole cemetery.

"Where were you?" asked the bride. "I've been looking for you."

"At the fountain and at the altars outside."

"Then I should have seen you."

"I wasn't long in any one place. I ran around. I had a look at everything."

"Thirsty!" cried the flute player and spat in a wide arc.

"Not now, this is the time to play," said the bride's father. "I paid you, how often do I have to say it?"

"I have no spit left," answered the flute player. "I can't play without spit. Money's no substitute for that."

"He's an old fox," said the groom's father. "He knows how to get what he wants. Give him something to drink, hell and damnation, we have to have music."

The bride's father motioned to his younger daughter. She went over to the women and fetched a jug of new wine. The old man gulped noisily and smacked his lips. Wasn't he ever going to set the jug down?

Sighing, he handed it back empty and said: "Will you invite me to your wedding too?"

"Yes," she answered.

"When are you going to get married, you pretty little woman?" He tickled her chin and ran his eyes over her thin, childish arms.

"In five years, when I'm sixteen," she said loudly.

He snorted.

"You needn't laugh," she said angrily, "I already have a fiancé, he's the handsomest and best of all of you."

"Did you hear that?" cried the old man and slapped his knee.

"Play, and don't slobber so much," the guitarist shouted at him.

The old man gave a start and put the flute to his lips. He had to strain to produce a note.

He won't last much longer, thought the guitarist. I'll have to look around for someone else. He used to be good, but now he's too old.

He sang two more songs, then he too motioned for the jug.

Soon he'll no longer know what he's singing, the mother thought, but his throat is reliable, I know him well, you can always dance to his songs, even when he's drunk.

The first candles were beginning to flicker on the graves. A couple of boys were kindling torches. But it wouldn't be long before the moon, already climbing up the cemetery wall, would be up, soon it would throw the shadows of the dancers across the graves.

"Don't you want to rise up and dance with us, Grandmother?" cried the bride's aunt. "It's still dark, you won't be recognized. And we won't even ask you who the fathers of your children were. Perhaps you'll find them living or dead, here in the cemetery."

136 |

"Be quiet," said the bride's father. "She was a good woman."

"Did I suggest anything else?" replied the aunt, laughing.

The crazy girl was wandering through the cemetery. In the course of the day she had learned her way around, and she was not afraid of the dark. She had left the wedding party, for the drum had terrified her, the wild dancing made her tremble. She had got as far as the rich people's cemetery without anyone noticing her absence. Down here, where brownish turf covered the graves, and hedges or fences surrounded them, where marble headstones and plaster statues loomed in the moonlight, it was peaceful. Here she felt comfortable.

There were only a few people strolling about among the candle-lit graves. Down the hillside, muffled by the dividing wall, the music drifted from the circles at the fountain and the crossing of the paths. The crazy girl watched a lady, the wife of the druggist in Marga-Marga, who was placing glasses over the candle flames. The crazy girl started to laugh and prattle.

"You get out of here," the woman said. "You belong up there."

The crazy girl did not understand. She liked being down here. She ran her hand over a crucified Christ and was enchanted by an angel that knelt on a pillar, weeping and pointing at a grave. She stroked its head, rose on tiptoe and traced the line of his lips with her finger.

People noticed her and drove her away. She ran a few steps, then ducked behind a headstone and waited. When she saw that no one was looking, she trotted on. Away from the central path, in the farthest, darkest corner of the rich people's cemetery, she suddenly came to the edge of an open grave, a freshly dug pit.

She shrank back in fright, but then she stepped forward again and stared, terrified but still curious, into the hole. The moonlight fell diagonally across the grave and lit one of its corners.

The crazy girl stretched out her arms and babbled. There lay her hat! Yes, it was her hat. She recognized it at once. The wind had blown it off her head, as she was walking to the fountain with her mother.

She knelt at the edge of the grave and bent over, but she could not reach it. She waved at a few people who were passing far away, but no one noticed her gesture, no one understood her plea.

So she acted on her own. Clawing with her hands at the clay on the edge, she let herself slide into the grave. Her feet did not reach all the way to the bottom, for she was small; she had to let herself drop. She rolled on her back, but got quickly to her feet again and rushed to the hat, which she picked up and smelled. She pressed it to her cheek, to her breast, shook it and blew the dust from it. As she patted it and put it on her head, she grunted with pleasure. Now she was quite and utterly satisfied.

But when she tried to climb out she realized she was trapped in this grave. She tried to claw her way up the walls, but her hands found no hold, the hard clay afforded no crevices for her feet. She wept and wailed, crawled mindlessly around the bottom of the pit, and finally beat the walls with her fists. The people in the rich people's cemetery looked at one another in surprise. Who could have lost someone so recently as to be overcome by such wild grief at his graveside?

But it was night, and even the moonlight revealed no one.

Manuel lifted his head and listened. He heard music. Now they were dancing. He staggered to his feet, stumbled a few steps, then he stopped to listen again. That was real music! What drumming! It grew louder and filled his ears, his temples, his whole head. He felt his way downhill, toward the noise of the booths. Into the cemetery, just not to be alone, into the music!

He groped past the booths. Near the entrance gate he met Don Eugenio, who moved out of his way and threw him a blank look. An old woman gave him a tortilla, and he accepted it because this old woman had given him a tortilla every year on All Souls' Day. She had been a friend of his mother's.

He did not see that she began to weep as he went off with the food.

"Such a handsome young man," she sobbed. "This can't turn out well. He'll never overcome it."

"He'll get used to it," the two women with whom she had been gossiping said comfortingly. "Can't one get used to everything? And the people will get used to him too, then everything will be all right again."

"You don't know him," said the old woman.

Manuel devoured the tortilla and then followed the voices of two men.

"Are you going to dance too?" one asked.

"Certainly. I'm going to join the group at the fountain. They have a good flute."

"But their drummer's no good. The one with the wedding party is better."

"I have relatives with the flute player."

"And I have relatives in the wedding party. Come along."

Manuel only had to follow their voices.

Suddenly he felt a hand touching his breast. "Excuse me, brother," said the hoarse voice of an old man. "Can you show me the way to the holy Emilio? I am blind. I've lost my way. There's such a crowd here!"

Manuel recoiled. Another blind man!

"Turn around and go the other way," he said at random. "The holy Emilio is buried over there."

"Just as I thought," cried the old man. "It's always so easy to lose your direction in a crowd. Are you going up there too by any chance?"

"Yes," Manuel said, without stopping to think.

"That's splendid!" cried the old man. "Would you mind if I held on to your poncho?"

"Do that. But we'll have to go slowly."

"That's all right, we blind people have a lot of time," said the old man and seized hold of Manuel's poncho. "May God repay you for your sympathy with the blind."

"Damn it," Manuel said, "I have no sympathy. It just happens that I'm going up that way, that's all."

"Don't deny your kind heart," gasped the old man. "I sense it."

If only he doesn't find out, thought Manuel. He strained his ears for the two voices that had been leading him. Once or twice he heard them in the distance, then they were drowned in the music and general murmuring. He let himself be carried along in the crowd for a way. They were walking steadily uphill. The music sounded nearer. It was the right direction.

"Have you been blind for long?" he asked.

"For thirty years now."

"And how did it happen?"

"Slaked lime, young man. Slaked lime, in both eyes."

"How do you make a living now?"

"I beg."

"I've never seen you around here."

"I don't live here. I'm from Potosi. But it's a good idea to change regions once in a while. I can tell you this: over in Potosi you can't count much on sympathy any more, they're used to me, but here you make out pretty well. One doesn't do badly at all, without eyes. You just have to put the right expression on your face, then it works."

"So that's how you do it," Manuel said.

"You can take my word for it: My wife has never been so well off as since the day when I was blinded, and the children too."

"But what about you?" Manuel asked. "How do you make out with everything so dark?"

"I can feel my wife just as well as before. I've given her three more since then. We had one before. But two died."

"That's not what I mean."

"Oh, you mean the darkness? Well, I dream a lot. That's how I make up for not seeing. All of them color dreams. Mostly round red suns and plump women and lots of green. I never saw that much green in all the years I could see. Funny, isn't it?"

"And you don't want to be able to see again?"

"Oh yes, I do," he said. "That's why I'm here, that's the reason I'm going to the holy Emilio. I have never seen my child, the youngest, the one that didn't die. It's a girl and they say she's blonde. Where the blondeness comes from the devil knows. She's said to be very cute, nine years old, she's called Albertina. Every time I come home she sits on my lap and kisses me over and over again. I would really love to see her. You know, I sometimes have the feeling that she's not mine because she's blonde. For a while my wife was a cleaning woman for a gringo, every Tuesday and Friday. You understand? I know the gringo, I know what he looks like. My wife claims it's all my imagination, but who can trust her?"

Manuel stumbled against a cross. So they had pushed him off the central path. He walked a few steps and ran into a second cross. Where were the noises of the people? He moved once more in their direction, and the old man followed him obediently, walked when he walked and stopped when he stopped. Manuel got back into the crowd, but now it was going downhill, that was the wrong direction, and he had to turn in a wide circle in order not to make the old man suspicious.

I ought to be beside the wall, Manuel thought. Then I could find the way.

"Don Emilio could do it," the old man went on chattering. "It's just his sort of thing. They tell the wildest stories about him in my town. He gave a woman of eighty a child, and a cow threw six calves at one time after she had been led around his grave. What are a pair of eyes compared to that?"

"I know nothing about it," Manuel said. "Have you any flowers?"

"No. Where would a blind man get flowers?"

"They say he won't do a thing without flowers."

"He is a saint. He'll do it out of pity. Who doesn't pity a blind man?"

"Look, those two blind men there!" whispered a child's voice close beside them.

"Tsst, you mustn't stare at them," a woman's voice replied.

Damn devil's brood, thought Manuel. Can't you keep your mouth shut? Now it's all over.

"Did you see them?" asked the old man.

"Who?"

"Why, the two blind men. Two blind men must have just gone by."

"Oh, those. Yes, I saw them."

"Are they from your town?"

"No, I don't know them."

"You don't suppose they intend to beg here too?"

"I don't think so."

"Dear God, those poor fellows," said a girl's voice in front of them. "Did you see that? Both blind."

"Two more blind men," the old man cried in excitement. "Strange, there seem to be a lot of blind people here. Can you explain that to me?"

"No," Manuel said.

"Perhaps they all live somewhere else and have also come here to beg? If they get in my way, they'll be sorry."

"Yes, make it hot for them," Manuel said, in order to say something.

"And you, my dear young friend, what do you do? Do you work in the mine?"

"I'm a waiter in the Hotel Atahualpa."

"Double blessings on your head! Then you're a made man, and I've been treating you familiarly!"

"Watch out where you step," Manuel said. "The ground is rough here."

They were approaching the fountain where the crowd was dancing. Manuel broke out in a sweat. How was he to get through? And wouldn't the people whisper again about the two blind men? Eventually the old man would be sure to catch on.

"Come, we'll make a detour," he said. "We'll circle around the dancers."

"Yes, yes," the old man nodded and fumbled obediently behind him.

Manuel stumbled over a cross.

"Hoopla," the old man cried merrily. "Seeing people can stumble too."

Manuel gritted his teeth. He felt in front of him with his hand. That drum! What were the two other drummers by comparison? Poor stutterers.

"Stay on the path, you two," said a woman and pushed against Manuel's leg. "You're walking on my bread!"

"It's so dark," Manuel answered. "You can't see anything."

"But don't the candles help? All those lights that we always have on All Souls' Day?" asked the old man.

"They don't give much light."

"Yes, it's taking us a long time to get there, but that

doesn't matter. The saints are ready to listen all night long."

Manuel walked faster. Over there was the fountain, from that direction came the second music, the one with the good flute. Emilio's grave was a little farther up.

"You'll burn your feet on the candles," said a man who was sitting on a mound. "If you're blind, why don't you get someone to lead you?"

"Only I am blind," called the old man. "Only I. With this young man everything is in fine working order!"

"Aha," the man said dryly.

"A couple of lights more or less don't matter," Manuel said hastily. "Why, the whole cemetery is full of them."

"It matters to the dead," the man replied. "You'll make them angry. You'd better take care. Where are you trying to go, anyway?"

"To Emilio," Manuel said. "I know the way."

"He's leading me," cried the old man. "He is so kind to me!"

The man took Manuel's hand and led him off the grave.

"Here's a small path. That's probably the one you mean?"

"Yes," said Manuel, "that's the one I mean. This is just the one I wanted to follow."

"It leads to the central path a short distance this side of Emilio's grave."

"That's the one. Many thanks!" called the old man. "People are kind here, I see it again and again," he said to Manuel. "A blessed region."

The talking and the music grew louder. Then the two were in the crowd on the central path again.

"Can you smell Emilio's candles now?" Manuel asked.

"Yes, indeed, I smell them," the old man said. "Now I can find my way alone in case you have something pressing to do. Don't let me hold you up! You have already done much too much. You've even let yourself be taken for a blind man for my sake!"

"Yes," Manuel said. "I have to go now. Goodby."

"Goodby," said the old man, feeling for Manuel's hand and shaking it in both of his. "I will pray to Emilio to keep your eyes safe."

Manuel began to laugh, but broke off abruptly.

"Yes," said the old man, "no one imagines it possible that he could become blind until it happens."

"Goodby," Manuel said again.

The old man pushed into the crowd around Emilio's grave. Manuel felt his way past and went on.

I must get to the wall, he thought.

He groped his way to it and leaned against it. From up here he would have been able to see all the lights. He pictured them to himself. But the music swept them out of his mind and drew him irresistibly on. The drum, the drum above all. The wall guided him, the musicians were not far from the wall, if he had not been blind he would only need to make a couple of jumps to be there with them and to join the dance. But now he dared not go farther. There must be light where they were dancing, he did not want them to see him, he wanted to remain in the darkness. Where did the light begin? How far did it reach?

Ten graves away from the music he stopped. He hummed, he swayed, finally in the darkness he began to

146 |

dance, hesitantly at first, then more freely. The path was wide, he ran into nothing. With outstretched arms he whirled to the rhythm of the song.

The bride's little sister saw his gyrating shadow as she stole along the upper wall, looking for him. She did not recognize him until she was passing close by. She gave a start and ducked, but then she remembered he could not see her and she stood up again.

He would like to dance, she thought. And why shouldn't he dance? I will help him.

"Manuel," she called softly.

He froze in the middle of a wild whirl and listened.

"Come over to us," she whispered. "Dance with me. I'll lead you. Before you run into anything I'll warn you. No one will notice that you can't see."

"Are you the little girl from the gate?"

"Yes. Come."

"But isn't that the wedding party that's dancing?"

"Just come, there are so many dancing. Who will recognize you?"

"But if they do recognize me they'll be angry. They don't like to see my face."

"But it's dark."

"It's never that dark where people are dancing. Have you torches, or is the moon shining?"

"It has just come up."

"If they see my eyes they'll remember the story. They hate it because it is true."

"I'll bring you a pair of glasses," the girl whispered. "I found them a few days ago, glasses with real lenses. My father offered them to Don Eugenio today, but he looked through them just once and laughed. Then Don

| 147

Leo bought them, the man who owns the lottery booth. He put them on right away, but soon he had to take them off again because his eyes had to get used to them, he said. The drummer told me about it. They let him look through them too, but he said he could hardly recognize anything at all. They're probably still lying there. In the dark, Don Leo won't notice if they're missing. You can wear them till you go home, then I'll put them back again. He certainly won't need them any more tonight."

"No," said Manuel. "I don't want them."

"But if you wore the glasses no one would recognize you, and if someone or other does recognize you they won't be terrified, for you can't see what is behind the glass. I'll go now and get them."

"Suppose Don Leo catches you?"

"He'll beat me. But what does that matter?"

"Suppose your father recognizes the glasses?"

"I'll tell him Don Leo loaned them to you."

"But I can't dance blind like this."

"You don't need to see, you only need to hear, then you can dance, and when the others see that they'll forget your face."

He didn't answer. She took his silence for agreement and ran off. Manuel stayed where he was, he was confused and didn't know if he should give in to this ridiculous child. But the music enticed him, it made him sick with longing, once more he whirled in a circle, humming the melody. Oh God, just to be able to dance to this music, to hear the drum and the stamping of feet!

The little girl came back. She had run down the slope and up again without stopping, she was strong, even though she was so thin.

"Here they are," she gasped.

He felt for the glasses and put them on.

"How do I look?" he asked.

"Very handsome. Very distinguished."

"I mean can you still see my eyes?"

"No one can see that you haven't any."

He let himself be drawn on by her, reluctant, yes, but full of secret desire.

He could already smell the sweat of the dancers and feel the earth tremble under his feet. The drum roared in his ears, the song shrilled. Everyone was singing along.

"No, I can't do it," he cried suddenly. "I can't dance with them. Let me go!"

She answered softly: "Don't you remember what it's like when you dance? Everyone bumps into everyone else. You won't be noticed in the crowd."

"But I can't see anything!"

"Just depend completely on me."

She tried to force him into the rhythm, took his groping hands and guided him cautiously to a place where the crowd was not too dense.

"I'm afraid of stepping on you," he said. "You are so small."

"I'll watch out," she replied. "I'll watch out for both of us."

He tried a few steps, and she saw how timid he was.

"See how well it's going," she whispered. "You're dancing like everyone else."

"I was always a good dancer. The girls were crazy about me, you can believe that!" he said.

The beat of the music caught him. He whirled the little girl around, he forced her to mighty leaps, she was so very light. When she fell, he let go of her, he pushed her away and danced alone. He spread his arms and threw his head back. His dancing became faster, wilder. People dancing near him noticed and made room for him.

"Come up here, monk, out of the Gran Chaco, and I'll show you what dancing means!" he cried. "Come up here, you Guaranis, look at this—I'm dancing in spite of you!"

"Isn't that Manuel?" asked the bride, shocked, and stopped dancing.

"He's wearing glasses," said the father of the bridegroom to the bride's father. "And I even believe they are yours!"

"Manuel," called the groom's mother, "you'll fall! Dance, but don't be so wild!"

He did not hear her. He groaned, he yelled, his voice cracked. It drowned out the guitarist, who broke off in the middle of his song. The dancing couples stumbled apart. With terror on her face, the bride's little sister shrank against the wall. She had brought courage to the blind man, but now he was out of control. Now he was happy, she saw it; he roared, he raved with happiness. But how would this dance end? Nobody dared to restrain him, not even her father.

The flute broke off, the guitar fell silent. Now only the drum accompanied the dancer, pounded, hacked, rolled; sweat ran down the drummer's forehead, he saw nothing but the blind man. His eyes sparkled, his mouth stretched open, his whole body quivered to the rhythm and the beat.

Manuel was now on Grandmother's grave. His poncho flew high and whipped around him, striking the faces of those nearest him. He threw his arms above his head and danced in wild leaps, faster and faster, he sang and sobbed.

The cross! He will fall over the grave cross! the small girl thought, full of dread. She darted toward Manuel and seized his poncho. But with a jerk he hurled her away.

"The cross!" screamed the guitarist.

Manuel heard no one. The circle of the wedding guests closed around him. All stared at the dancer. When would he fall?

"Manuel!" cried the little one.

"Stop drumming," the bride's father commanded the drummer, but he also heard nothing. His hands whirled above the drum, accelerating the fiery rhythm, his eyes, full of wonder, were fastened to the dancer on the grave.

At that instant Manuel stumbled against the cross and fell full length. The glasses were jerked from his face and flew in a high arc into the crowd.

The drummer, exhausted, let his hands drop, and then in the silence that followed, burst into childish laughter! A dancer had stumbled and fallen. That had always been grounds for laughter. But when he realized that he was the only one laughing, he fell silent, looked around and saw unsmiling faces.

The bride's small sister saw only Manuel. She tried to run to him, to help him up, but someone held her back. She watched Manuel slowly raise himself to a crouch and grope for the tin wreath, run into the cross and tear the tin wreath off. Even as a shriek of dreadful foreboding rose to her lips, Manuel threw himself on the drummer, blindly following the direction of the laughter, and smashed the wreath over his head.

The drummer, stiff with terror, made no attempt to defend himself or get away. He stood and let the blows fall on him until the blood streamed down his face. The bridegroom lunged at Manuel from behind, but he hurled him off. The drummer sank to his knees. When Manuel realized he was beating the empty air, he threw the wreath into the crowd, which drew back screaming, felt for the drummer, seized the youngster's thin neck in both hands and began to choke him.

Now the drummer tried to fight back, he reared back and struck out with both arms. Manuel plunged down upon him, the drum rolled rattling against the wall, bounced off and hit the feet of the little girl.

Women screamed. A child began to wail. The guttering torches illuminated only Manuel and the drummer who lay helpless beneath him. The drummer's face was swollen and blue-red, he gasped, emitted a strange, high sound and then was still.

Now the bride's two brothers threw themselves on Manuel, but the blind man would not release his grip. He kicked out. He struck the elder brother in the face, the younger in the groin. His face, contorted with rage, hung over the lifeless face of the young man. The guitar player tore the cross from the grandmother's grave and began to beat Manuel with it. Manuel did not let go, but fastened his hands more furiously around the drummer's neck. The body beneath him arched once more, then went slack. Only the fingers still moved. The wedding party stared in fascination at the scrabbling, twitching fingers, until the bride's father threw himself on Manuel and got his hands around his throat. Overpowered, Manuel let go of the boy's throat.

The two brothers hauled Manuel to his feet. The drummer lay there and moved no more. His eyes were wide open. The groom's father crouched down and bent over him. The wedding party pressed closer. Those who had been standing in the rear had not been able to see the men on the ground and now wanted to know what was happening. Children edged toward the front of the circle, and one of them trod the glasses into the earth.

"I guess you've had enough now, eh?" Manuel gasped, his whole body shaking. "Now I guess you won't be able to laugh at me for a while, you mangy son of a bitch."

"Yes, you've fixed that," answered the bride's older brother. "He won't laugh at you any more, he'll never laugh at you again, you can count on that, it's over and done with forever. You've done a thorough job, Manuel."

Manuel raised his head.

After a while he asked, "Is he dead?"

"Yes."

"Who was it?"

"The drummer."

"The drummer laughed at me?"

"Yes, that's who it was. The way a child laughs. A boy of fifteen."

Manuel threw his head back and hissed derisively.

"Whoever laughs at me must pay for it," he shouted.

A shadow was approaching.

"Put out the torches," the bride's father said softly. "The gendarme is coming."

The torches were extinguished, a few men squatted around the body. The moon had just climbed over the wall. In its pale light a gendarme appeared between the graves.

"Why have you put out the torches?" he asked.

"The moon gives enough light," the groom's father said. "We haven't many torches. We have to save them."

"And why aren't you dancing?"

"We've had enough for a while. We're resting. Later, we'll go on."

"You were singing very loud. Don't get too excited, or knives will flash."

"We'll be quieter."

"And no trading."

"Why should we do that? We're a wedding party. Here is the bride, there the groom."

"My congratulations," said the gendarme. He bent over and picked up a pocket mirror that was gleaming in the moonlight. "Did one of you lose this?" he asked.

"It belongs to me," the flute player replied and stepped forward.

"You ought to take better care of your treasures," said the gendarme. He handed the mirror to the flute player and departed.

"What now?" the mother asked. She could hardly stand, her knees were trembling so.

"That boy has a mother," said the flute player. "In Huapi, four doors this side of the slaughterhouse. Pedro, you have a donkey."

"Yes," said Pedro, a cousin, who had also come from Huapi. "I have a donkey, and I'll take him back on it if I have to, but someone must come with me. I'd be scared to be alone with a dead person. The dead draw the devil."

"But not this one. He was still completely innocent."

154 |

"I'll go with you, Pedro," the bride's father said. "We'll leave it to his mother whether she wants to bring charges against Manuel or not. But I don't believe she will. If the people ask, it was an accident, an unlucky fall in the dark on top of a cross, or something of that sort. You who were here keep quiet. And you, Manuel, go away. We won't give you away, but go away."

Manuel turned his head and asked: "Where is the wall?"

The groom's father took his arm and led him to it. Manuel was silent, and no one could read in his face what he was thinking, for the wall threw a moon shadow where he stood. In the darkness of this shadow he slowly groped his way off.

The bride's little sister stood with her mouth open, unable to take in what had happened. Her eyes were fixed on the drum at her feet. While the men wrapped the dead boy in his poncho, she picked up the drum, pressed it to her breast with both hands and stood staring after Manuel.

"But we'll have to do something," said the bride. "We can't just sit here and pretend that nothing has happened! And yet we can't go on drinking and celebrating and dancing!"

"Why not?" asked her father. "He won't come back to life. It's over with him."

"The best thing would be for us to go on dancing," the bridegroom replied. "It would attract attention if we stopped now."

"But we have no drummer," said the guitarist. "Even the gendarmes will notice that something's wrong with the music if we go on playing now."

"Maybe someone else knows how to drum?"

The guitarist shook his head and smiled wearily.

"It's not so easy to substitute for that drummer. I discovered him. He really knew his job. He could drum all the others to the wall. If they hear someone else, they'll all come and ask why he's not here. A miserable thing about that youngster."

"Don't forget the button," the old flute player said. "He won it today, it must be in his pants pocket. He wanted to give it to his mother. And here is the mirror too. It belongs to him."

"We ought to go home," said the bride.

"That's true," said the groom's mother. "My son has to leave early tomorrow. Everyone will understand if we don't spend the whole night here."

"No!" cried the guitarist. "That would make people wonder. No sensible person who is healthy and old enough goes home at this hour on All Souls' Day."

"And I don't want to, either," said the groom. "Not now. Especially not now."

"You're right," said the bride's aunt. "We haven't been to Uncle's grave yet. You weren't not planning to visit him? He's the bride's uncle! Do you want him to pursue you with evil wishes for celebrating a wedding here on All Souls' Day without visiting him? You all know what sort of man he was. He was something special. He could do you great harm if you insult him. Think of the Gran Chaco!"

"Yes, yes," said the bride. "That's true. We must not anger him. We'll have to pay him a visit."

They squatted in a circle and looked at one another helplessly, while the bride's father loaded the dead man

156 |

on his shoulder and walked off across the graves with his younger son and Pedro.

"What will you say if someone asks what you're carrying?" Pedro asked him.

"Skins," replied the bride's father, "that I've just bought. And then I'll walk on quickly. I'll say that I'm in a hurry."

They moved off between the crosses. The wedding party looked after them until they disappeared into the night.

"The poor devil," murmured the mother. "Murdered, strangled like a young kitten. And all because he laughed."

"Just be quiet, he'll go to heaven," her husband said.

"But he's dead!"

"No one goes to heaven alive, not even Jesus Christ."

"And what good is that to his mother, his going to heaven? She is here, and he is there!"

"Just stop it now," said the groom's father angrily. "As though it were something peculiar for a man to be killed. You know it yourself: something happens every year on All Souls' Day, and this time it turned out to be the drummer. That's all there is to it."

"Yes, yes, it wasn't your son!"

"It wouldn't have happened to him. He'd have knocked his teeth in, and some other things besides."

"You should have held on to him!" the mother said stormily.

"But you know how crazy he is, that Manuel!"

"Didn't you see how we tried? Even your own son

tackled him. But it was as though he'd gone crazy, he's strong as a bull!"

"Yes indeed," whispered a young woman, "like a bull. He snorted like a bull."

"He is crazy!" the mother shouted.

"If you're not quieter I'll hit you right here in front of everybody!" hissed the bridegroom's father. "The idea, making so much noise! Do you want us all to end up in jail?"

The mother began to weep. "A madman," she wailed. "And he walks around free and terrifies people with that face and strangles children! If you don't look out he'll strangle your own children, your son and your daughter too. And you just stand there and look on!"

"This will show you how I look on," he said and struck her in the face with the flat of his hand.

She fell silent immediately and crossed her arms in front of her head. But he hit her only once. Slowly she let her hands fall. Then she suddenly stood up and peered around.

"Don't attract attention," her husband said. "They'll get through the gate all right. You know they've wrapped him in his poncho, and he is small and thin."

"Our crazy girl is gone," the mother replied.

But his thoughts were on the drummer. He did not hear her.

"She is gone!" the mother cried and seized him by the sleeve.

Now he also got up. He called softly to his daughter, but there was no answer.

"You see, she's gone," the mother said. "She's creeping about somewhere in the darkness, and if he falls over her he'll get angry and beat her to death. Then you can comfort yourself with the thought that she'll go to heaven!"

"Has anyone seen her?" asked the father.

No one had seen her.

"We'll look for her," the guitarist said. "We'll all search for her together. That's the best excuse. That's why we're not dancing any more, you understand? We'll divide up and search the whole cemetery. If anyone asks us what's become of the drummer—what do we know? He must be searching too."

"When we find her, we'll meet at Uncle's grave," the father whispered. "Don't forget, at the grave of the bride's uncle. Up there, you know the place."

The wedding guests nodded.

"And if she won't come?" asked the bride's older brother. "She can be very stubborn."

"Then call me."

"Where shall we find you?"

"I'll stand at the gate so that she can't run out."

The people got up and hurried off among the graves. Only the bride's little sister still stood there with the drum in her hands and did not move.

"Good God, the drum!" cried the groom's father when he caught sight of her. "Are you crazy? Holding that up where anyone can see it! It will give everything away. Give it to me. I'll hide it in one of the bundles."

The little one only stared at him, full of dread, and clasped the drum even tighter. When he tried to take it away from her, she ran off with it.

Carrying the dead man out, they had to avoid the central path, for the second group of musicians were playing at the fountain and the third at the crossing of the paths. Crowds had collected in both places. The dances being played made a confused dissonance, one of them hurrying ahead and intruding its shrill notes on the slower beat of the other. The bride's father became as confused as the music and stumbled over the graves.

"Our music was the best," said he.

They crossed the poor people's cemetery, then that of the rich and arrived unmolested at the entrance.

"Let me first see where the gendarme is sitting," whispered the bride's younger brother to his father, who was carrying the drummer.

He peered out the gate. The gendarme was sitting at a distance from the entrance, leaning his back against the wall and with his eyes closed. A small fire in front of him illuminated his face.

"You can go now," said the younger brother.

They carried the body out, and in the shadow of a cart they tied it on Pedro's donkey. But now it was clear that those were not skins rolled up on the donkey's back.

"Soused to the gills, eh?" said a man who was staggering past.

"Yes, absolutely soused," murmured the bride's father. "We're taking him home."

"Doesn't matter, doesn't matter," the man babbled. "He'll get over it. After all, this is All Souls' Day. Anyone who doesn't get soused isn't a man. *Ego te absolvo*."

So saying, he fell to the ground and began to snore.

"Go back into the cemetery," the father whispered to his son. "Otherwise they'll ask your brother where you are. People are used to always seeing you two together. Pedro and I will take care of this. In two hours I'll be back."

The son nodded and disappeared into the cemetery. The donkey trotted out onto the plain, white in the moonlight. The edges of the poncho that covered the drummer dragged in the grass.

VIII

MANUEL FELT HIS WAY ALONG THE WALL. HE KNEW that this way would eventually lead him to the gate. The wall was no longer deserted. He stumbled over drunks, who growled at him angrily, over sleepers and lovers.

"Open your eyes, you idiot!" a young fellow shouted at him angrily.

"Lie down and sleep it off," said an old woman whose hand he had stepped on.

He ignored the nagging. He wanted to reach the gate, and he had to reach the gate, nothing else mattered.

"You can't get through here," a woman said and braced herself against him. "There are children sleeping here."

"Don't touch me!"

"I'll lead you around on the outside."

"Leave me alone!" he muttered and pushed himself away from the wall. He carefully groped his way around the children until he reached the wall again.

"Lucky for you you didn't step on them," the woman muttered after him. "I'd have scratched your eyes out."

162 |

Manuel laughed out loud.

"My God, what a laugh you have," said the woman. "It makes one's blood run cold."

After all, what have I done? Manuel asked himself as he fumbled on. Is a murder so unheard of? This isn't my first by any means. In the beginning I went all to pieces, that first time I knifed a man. He writhed on the ground and screamed for a long while, and then he just kept rattling. If he had opened his eyes and looked at me, O gracious Virgin of Copacabana, he would have burst his sides laughing, for I was cowering there beside him with the silliest look on my face and was paralyzed with terror. Yes, I even vomited, right next to him, but he didn't see that, by that time he was already dead. Later I didn't give a damn. Once I even took care of eight in a single day.

And that one there? I don't even know what he looks like. He deserved what he got, he laughed at me because I stumbled. No one laughs at me and gets away with it. They all found that out tonight, everyone who saw it, and I'll make sure that all of Marga-Marga is afraid of me. I'll put an end to their pity once and for all. I don't want them to keep their mouths shut because they're sorry for me. And I don't want his mother to protect me. What happens to me is my business and nobody else's. Damn their pity!

"There you are!" called a child's voice behind him. Someone pulled at his poncho.

"Who's that?" he asked and whirled around.

"It's me. I looked for your eyes in the fountain today while it was still light."

"Oh yes, you . . ."

"But they weren't in the fountain, and when I came back to tell you you had gone."

"Come here, Pepe," called a woman.

"That's my mother," the boy said. "But first tell me whether you have seen them."

"Who?"

"Why, your eyes! They're still not in your face."

Manuel stopped and smiled tiredly.

"They didn't come back at all. Not in the afternoon and not in the evening."

"Maybe they crept into someone else's head."

"Come here at once, child!" the woman called.

"But after all you can't run around this way without eyes," the boy said. "You can't see anything and you'll stumble over the people."

"Yes, it's quite a bore to have to go around blind this way."

"That's mean of them—to run away and not come back."

"Perhaps someone caught them."

"I kept looking for you the whole time, for I had seen you sitting here by the wall. But then when I got back you had gone. What have you been doing since then?"

"All sorts of things."

"Searching?"

"Yes."

The boy was deep in thought.

"I have to go now," Manuel said. "And thanks for helping me look."

"Now will you buy a pair of new ones?"

"I have no money."

"But you can't stay without eyes!"

"Pepe," called the woman. "Where the devil are you?"

"I'll manage," Manuel said and hurried on. The boy ran beside him.

"Suppose I gave you one of mine? I have two, you know."

"That wouldn't work," Manuel said. "You have child's eyes, after all, and the ones I lost were man's eyes. Your eyes would fall out of my head, because they're too small."

"Yes," the boy said sadly, "that's true."

But he still did not let go of Manuel's poncho.

"Anyway, if I find your eyes I'll bring them to you," he said.

"Pepe, Pepe," the woman shrieked.

"Yes, that would be good."

"I've got to go now," the boy said. "Just don't be sad. If you want me, my name is Pepe and I live in Huapi."

"Thanks," Manuel said.

He felt the hand let go of his poncho, and listened to the pattering footsteps.

"Come a little farther with me," he called softly.

"Did you say something?" the boy called.

"No," said Manuel.

More and more candles flickered on the graves. A beautiful night, no wind! There was hardly any need to shield the flames. The cemetery lay like the mirror of a starry sky in the middle of the black field of the plain. Far up the hillside countless lights were crowded together on a single grave. There lay Emilio under his flowers.

The bride's little sister had spied Manuel and overtaken him. She was panting, for the drum was heavy and made it hard for her to run.

| 165

"Where are you going, Manuel?" she asked, trotting along beside him.

He recognized her voice.

"Go back to your people. Leave me alone."

"Do you want me to lead you?"

"You're sorry for me, aren't you? Go to hell!"

"They'll all keep quiet about it," she whispered.

"What do I care? I don't need their help. I do what I want."

She kept following him, even though he said nothing more to her. He heard her light footsteps behind him.

"Devil's dung!" he hissed and turned around. "Can't you leave me in peace, you repulsive little beast?"

She stopped, shocked. He groped his way off. She stood and looked after him, and still held the drum clutched in both arms. A filthy dog circled around her, rubbed against her and poked the drum with his snout. The drum rolled rattling downhill somewhere among the graves. The girl knelt down and pulled the dog to her. He began licking her face with his long tongue.

Standing at the gate, the groom's father saw Manuel going by. He's leaving the cemetery, he thought. That's good. He'll go home. The thing can be hushed up. And the drummer's mother won't go to the police. None of us will go to the police. The murderer is blind, what could they find out if they arrested him? And besides, why should the police make a fuss about the death of one poor soul, especially in wartime?

He leaned against the side of the wall and stared at the central path. Where could she be, that confounded crazy daughter of his?

He lifted his head and listened. He heard someone crying, quite softly and far away. How strange that anyone in the cemetery should be weeping this late on All Souls' Day when the festival had reached its high point and the people up there were dancing. Hadn't there been enough time for tears during the day, if anyone had to weep?

He kept on listening but could not hear it now, for the noise of the buyers and sellers in front of the cemetery swelled, and on the hillside the musicians were playing.

Manuel found his way through the gate and stopped. One of the two gendarmes must be here, either to the right or the left of the gate. Where had they always sat? He could no longer remember exactly. But he knew from earlier years that one of them kept watch out here, the other made the rounds inside. At the end of each hour they changed off. And the one who sat out here had the advantage of being able to warm himself at the fire. For they wore uniforms, not ponchos.

Manuel went along the wall, first to the right, then to the left, but he did not find the warmth of the fire. Finally he asked a man who brushed against him, "Hey there, do you see the gendarme anywhere around?"

The man was taken aback and threw a quick look at Manuel. The moonlight fell full on the blind face. Then the man understood Manuel's question.

"The corporal's sitting over there by the wall, almost at the corner. Shall I take you to him?"

"I'll find him myself," Manuel replied.

He stumbled over boxes and crates. As he fell he reached out for a handhold and was rudely hauled back just as he felt the heat of the fire on his face.

"Sleepyhead, watch what you're doing! Or do you want to lie in the fire and be roasted?" cried a man's voice.

Manuel made no reply and offered no thanks. Now he went cautiously on around the edge of the heat.

"Corporal?" he whispered.

"What is it?" the gendarme replied, drunk with sleep.

"I strangled someone."

The gendarme opened his eyes wide.

"Don't tell fairy tales," he said. "You're drunk."

"But it's true, by the Virgin of Copacabana!"

"And who will you have strangled?"

"I don't know him, they say he was a musician, a drummer."

The gendarme got up and only then recognized Manuel. Everyone in Marga-Marga knew him. He grinned.

"Oh, it's you, Manuel."

He was about to sit down again.

"I've just told you I strangled someone," Manuel repeated loudly.

"Go home and tell it to your grandmother," said the gendarme.

"Do you want me to swear it again?"

"You, Manuel, strangled a man? How did you find his neck?"

"I grabbed for it, and then I got hold of it and didn't let go till he was dead."

"Are you sure he's dead?"

"Lots of people saw it. They said he was dead."

"And what's your reason for having doing it?"

"He laughed at me because I stumbled."

The gendarme did not know what to make of it. A blind man had strangled someone who could see, a crazy

168 |

business, if it was true. But it sounded like a damn fraud. This Manuel was a strange fellow, way off the rails, you never knew what he had up his sleeve. But to strangle someone, just because he had laughed? Nevertheless, he would have to look into the matter, otherwise he'd get in trouble.

He threw a sad look at the fire. It had been so comfortable there. And he had been hoping that this night would pass without incident. Now he had to chase off into the cold cemetery.

"Jesus," he said. "Couldn't you pick some other day for your nonsense? Stay here till I come back."

"Aren't you afraid I'll run away?" Manuel asked in amazement.

"You?" the gendarme laughed. "Sit by the fire and enjoy it. It might as well do somebody some good."

Manuel, full of hatred, listened to his retreating steps. This one didn't believe him either. No one believed him. But he would prove it. The gendarme had gone off into the crowd. The sound of his footsteps faded away. That imbecile of a gendarme, he had no notion at all whether he had a murderer in his hands or not.

Manuel spat into the fire.

The corporal strode through the gate into the cemetery.

The first corpse for this night, if the story's true, he thought. Last year there were two. Nuisances, nothing but nuisances, and for nothing.

"Hey you," he shouted to a figure retreating out of the moonlight and into the shadow of the wall. "Aren't you the groom's father?"

"Yes, corporal."

"You had a drummer with you when you came to the cemetery?"

"Yes, corporal, we hired him for All Souls' Day."

"Where is he now?"

"How do I know?"

"Where is the dead man?"

"What dead man?"

"The drummer."

"The drummer is dead? Jesus Maria!"

"Don't pretend. You've known it all along."

"I? How should I know that?"

"You were with him the whole time."

"I saw him with my own eyes a short while ago. We stopped dancing because my daughter disappeared. You know, the crazy one. The drummer is probably searching too. How do I know where he is at this moment? And who is supposed to have killed him?"

"Manuel."

"The blind man? Did he tell you that himself?"

"He's just been with me."

"How can a blind man strangle someone who can see?"

"How do you know he was strangled?"

The groom's father was rattled for a moment and then quickly said, "How else could Manuel do it? He was with us for a bit earlier, and I saw he had no knife with him."

"I don't trust you," said the corporal. "It's always the same with all of you. You shut your mouths with seven locks, even when you talk."

"If you happen to see my daughter, be so kind as to let me know. You know that she's crazy," said the groom's father. He bowed and went back to his position against the wall.

The corporal turned and walked away.

"That's just like him," murmured the groom's father, shaking his head. "So full of pride. Goes and informs against himself."

The corporal knew all the people of Marga-Marga, even the children, for he had been in service there for twenty-seven years, although he had originally come from Huapi. He found the bride's small sister sitting by the path that ran along the edge of the wall.

"Aren't you the bride's little sister?" he asked her.

"Yes, sir."

Startled, she took her arms from around the dog. The cur leaped up and barked at the gendarme.

"Did you see Manuel strangle the drummer?"

She did not move or speak. The dog yelped. The corporal kicked at him and said, "Hey girl, admit it, you were there."

The small one was silent.

I've frightened her, thought the gendarme. After all, she's only a child. Perhaps she really doesn't know anything, perhaps she's just hearing it for the first time from me, and if none of this is true she'll get another shock: if she meets the two of them again.

"All right, all right," he said, and turned away.

He crossed the cemetery. The groom's mother bustled past him near the fountain.

"Why are you running so?" he asked her, standing in her way.

"I'm looking for my daughter."

"Did you see the drummer get strangled?"

The mother gave a start.

"Strangled?" she whispered. "I don't know anything about it. Let me go, I'm looking for my daughter."

"I won't let you go until you tell me where the drummer is."

"How should I know? Ask my husband. He knows the answers to everything. I'm looking for my daughter."

"But you must have seen the drummer! You were there when he was drumming."

"I have seen nothing and I wasn't there at all. I'm looking for my daughter."

He let her run off. She was a woman. You couldn't do much with her.

The two musicians stood at Emilio's grave, their heads bowed low over folded hands, deep in prayer, waiting for the gendarme, whom they had seen standing with the bridegroom's mother.

"Where's your third, the drummer?" the corporal asked.

The two barely glanced up. They took their time answering, for they were praying. Finally they crossed themselves and lifted their heads.

"What was that, corporal?" said the guitarist.

"Don't be a fool," the corporal replied. "You heard me right."

"The drummer? We don't know. Maybe he's gone home already."

"How come? Weren't you going to go on playing?"

"They're looking for the mad girl and so they aren't dancing any more."

172 |

"And if they find her? What will you do without him?"

"Maybe he's still around. Who knows? Perhaps he's searching too."

"Did you see him with Manuel?"

"Manuel watched us while we were playing. Afterward he went away."

"Did he speak to the drummer?"

"Perhaps he said a few words to him, perhaps not. Who knows, corporal? When we're playing we don't see much of anything."

The corporal had no real desire to continue his investigation. He looked for his comrade and found him near the fountain in a circle of drinkers.

"You're not drinking too, by any chance?" he asked, when he had called him aside.

"Of course not. But if everyone around you is drinking you smell of liquor yourself. And you? Shouldn't you be out by the fire?"

The corporal told the story. He no longer believed it himself.

"It's difficult with these people," he said. "One can't get close to them. They don't want to have anything to do with us. Whatever you ask them, they're evasive. You can't get anything out of them."

"Filthy folk."

"Did you notice anything?"

"They were dancing up there," said the second gendarme. "Now they're gone. Let's just go up and look around."

The two brothers were sitting on Grandmother's grave talking quietly with each other. They had washed the wreath and strewn sand over the blood on the mound. They had also found the eyeglasses and cleaned them. They weren't broken.

The bride's aunt came running. "Manuel has informed against himself," she whispered. "And now the gendarmes are going around asking questions. They'll be after you too, be careful."

"Don't worry," answered the younger brother. "We'll make out with them all right."

The aunt disappeared among the graves.

"So he's given himself away," said the older one.

"Such an idiot," said the younger. "Now we'll have to be doubly careful."

They were silent for a while, then the older one said, "Will we stay together down there, do you think?"

"They're sure to leave brothers together. Have you ever heard of their separating brothers?"

"Earlier I would have preferred being alone. Because you're smarter than I am. That makes it hard for me. You can do everything better, and everyone likes you better than me. But down there I'd rather be with you. It's safer."

"Maybe they'll ask us whether we want to stay together or not. And if we want to, then they'll let us."

"Do you think so?"

"Certainly."

When they saw the gendarmes coming, they fell silent.

"Why don't you go on talking?" the corporal asked. "Are you scared because we're here?"

"We had just finished with what we were talking about."

174 |

"About Manuel?"

"Why about him?"

"That's what we'd like to know from you."

"We were talking about the Chaco," said the older brother.

"Is there something you'd like to know about Manuel?" asked the younger. "Are you having trouble with him?"

"You might say that," replied the second gendarme.

"He's having another of his crazy days."

"What do you mean by crazy days?" asked the corporal cautiously.

"He's boasting to high heaven about what he can do and who he is. Has he tried to put something over on you?"

"He says he strangled the drummer," said the second gendarme.

"Be quiet!" the corporal shouted at him.

The younger brother laughed.

"And you believe him? All he cares about is being the center of attention, even if it costs him a lot. He'd even let himself be put in jail if he had to."

The corporal turned on his heel and left. Disconcerted, the second gendarme looked after him, but there was nothing to do but follow him. The two brothers grinned at each other.

"He's given it up," said the younger.

"Would you ever have guessed that Manuel would turn himself in?" asked the older.

"It's like him. I don't know what one should wish for him. If they believe his story, it will cost him a couple of years, and if they don't believe it then he'll keep on with his mad ways."

"What can they actually prove? They won't find any witnesses to testify, and Manuel is blind. He saw no one."

"And if they look for the drummer?"

"Then he's gone to La Paz. Now in wartime there's so much else on their minds. They won't waste much time over that youngster. He's not of any importance to them."

They got up and crossed the field of black crosses. The bridegroom met them.

"Have you found the crazy one?" asked the younger brother.

"No. And how did it go with you? The gendarmes were talking to you."

"They no longer believe the story. Who would believe someone like Manuel?"

"And yet it's true," whispered the bridegroom. "Today was the first time I've ever seen anything like that. It was horrible. I don't believe I could do it. And you? Could you strangle someone?"

"They say you quickly get used to it," answered the younger brother. "Besides, it won't be people from Marga-Marga that we have to kill."

"They say the Guaranis come running at you with knives in their teeth and knives in their hands," said the older brother. "And I have to admit that I'm scared of snakes. I've never seen one, but I have a horror of them. Such a little brute, and yet it can settle your hash for good."

"You have to hack their heads off when they strike at you, people say," remarked the bridegroom. "But what do I do if a Guarani springs at me? Shall I hack off his head too, like an animal? But if I don't do it, then he'll hack off mine. So I've got to."

"I'm curious, that's all," said the younger brother. "We'll get used to it all right."

"But what if we die?" asked the other.

"What does it matter? Have you done much evil?"

"I don't think so."

"Me neither. Anyway nothing I'd have to go to hell for. A couple of weeks of purgatory, then paradise. Only the first moment, that will hurt a bit, but once you get used to it—"

"Just the same, I don't want to be dead," said the bridegroom. "Before it didn't matter much, but now I'm against it because I'm married. My father will beat her. She says she doesn't want to sleep near my sister. There will be quarrels. I have to come back soon. Besides, we want to have a lot of children."

A procession of hats was silhouetted by the moonlight. Hundreds of hats along the middle path, around the fountain, at Emilio's grave, along the wall. The lights on the graves were flickering low and some had already gone out. But outside, in front of the gate, the people were thronging around the candle sellers. The graves would gleam until dawn.

The section of children's graves now seemed very much bigger, for the crosses there shimmered white in the darkness. At the crossing of the paths people were still dancing, but at the fountain they were already drinking. Children darted among the graves, dogs rushed after them.

"I would like to go back," whispered the bridegroom.

IX

"WE FOUND HER," SAID THE BRIDE'S AUNT TO THE BRIDE-groom's father, who was still leaning beside the gate. "Down there, not far away, in Señorita Marisol's grave, hunched up and staring up at us. Poor thing. Who knows how long she'd been there? If she weren't mad already, I think this would have been enough to send her off. Like a mouse in a trap!"

"She's a cross to us. But she's here, and that's all there is to it."

"They're all already on their way to Uncle Lazaro's grave. Come along. We're going to drink, the way we always do on All Souls' Day. But this time we'll drink to eternal bliss for the drummer."

She seized his arm and led him up the slope.

O sweet Virgin of Copacabana, the mother thought, and tenderly looked at the crazy girl, who was stumbling beside her with tear-drenched face, you have protected her and held your hand over her. She is my only daughter, and in this moonlight no one can see that she is mad. Now she looks like any other girl. She has pretty hair, she has soft skin. She is my only daughter. What difference does it make that she is crazy?

Yes, what an uncle he had been! Because of him the worth of his niece, the bride, was enhanced. When his children were grown and able to earn their own living, he had suddenly sold two of his llamas, given the rest of the herd to his children, wandered with a little money to Oruro, and had there bought a ticket and traveled to Uyoni. In that town he had met some Indios who were planning to go farther. So he traveled with them for a day and a night in a railroad train, across mountains and valleys and around volcanic craters, all the way down to the Chilean wasteland of Atacama. The train, which was supposed to continue on to Antofagasta, had broken down at the oasis of Calama. And so Lazaro stopped there too, who had had no idea what the final destination of this trip was or even the name of the place. He took things as they came, and he stayed in Calama about a year, working in the copper mine that lay the barren heights above the city.

On his grave the wedding party was now slowly assembling. He had been the pride of the family, a man who had seen the world. How could one leave the cemetery without visiting him? The wedding celebration was to end with him.

The crazy girl laid her head in her mother's lap and clung to her skirts. She shivered at every movement the mother made; staring up at her, her wide eyes mirroring the moon, she followed her mother's every move.

"Unpack," said the bride's aunt. "We're thirsty, after all that."

"Yes, thirsty," shouted the flute player. "I'm going to drink until dawn. I'm going to drink myself full as an ox at the trough."

The women produced jugs from shadowy baskets and bundles. Round-bellied bottles glinted in the moonlight, drops of wine fell on Uncle Lazaro's grave. In the midst of the moonlit area the dark figures of the wedding party crouched and drank. After a while the little sister crept up and huddled beside the bride.

"Where have you been?" asked the bride softly.

"What does it matter to you?" the little girl answered, even more softly.

The bride made no reply. She held out the jug. The little one took it, put it to her lips and drank until the bride pulled it away from her.

"Are you crazy? That's not water, you know."

The little girl propped her chin on her fists. Full of hate, she listened to the aunt's first coy laughter.

"The gendarmes suspect something," she said. "Have they found out?"

"Just imagine," the bride said, "Manuel turned himself in!"

The little one looked at her with big eyes.

"He went down to the gendarme and told him. He betrayed himself."

The little one made no reply.

"What do you say to that?" asked the bride. "Would you ever have expected that? He did it just to make us angry."

"What are they going to do to him?" asked the

little girl in a strained voice. "Will they shoot him?"

"If they only would. I'd love to watch! But they don't believe any of it. They think he just wants to make himself important."

"Did they question you too?"

"Not me, but the others."

"And if they ask you if it's true—what would you say?"

"Nothing. The gendarmes have no business butting in."

"They don't believe him," said the girl. "That's wonderful. I like those men, the two gendarmes."

The bridegroom's father motioned the girl to him. She obeyed.

"Where did you leave the drum?" he asked softly.

The small one pointed into the darkness.

"Go and get it," he whispered. "Put it under your poncho and don't let anyone see it. You simply left the drum lying around! Can't you use your brains a bit? After all, you're eleven, almost twelve, you ought to be able to understand that no one must see the drum!"

The little one walked slowly off.

"Run!" he shouted after her.

But she did not run.

Except for the heat in Calama the uncle might have stayed much longer, for things went well with him there. He lived with another Bolivian Indio outside the city in a hut which they put together from cartons and gasoline cans, and he earned enough to be well satisfied. He could even give part of his earnings to an Indian girl who slept with him from time to time. But during the day the desert was hellishly hot. Why not move to the cool south? When he heard about a Madonna of Andacollo who was said to be enthroned in a cathedral down there, nothing could hold him back. One day he did not show up for work at the mine and went to Antofagasta. There, for the first time in his life, he saw the sea.

For almost a year he begged his way from one coast town to another, as far south as Coquimbo. There he knew he was not very far from the Madonna. Her church must be somewhere in the mountains above the city.

Manuel heard the corporal coming back and raised his head.

"Well, now do you believe it?" he asked.

"You could have spared me that job," the corporal said angrily and sank down beside him.

"What do you mean by that?"

The corporal leaned back and closed his eyes.

"I ran through the entire cemetery and made a laughing stock of myself just because you like to play first fiddle! Don't try that again. We could arrest you."

"So you don't believe I strangled the drummer?" Manuel asked and bent forward.

The corporal grinned.

"You probably believe it yourself, don't you?"

"Don't you think I could do it?"

"Before, yes."

"But not now?"

The corporal put his hand on Manuel's shoulder.

"Let me tell you something. In the long run you won't be able to make out, the way you're going now. You're a stout fellow, and everyone would like to like you—

because of before. But that won't last long. You offend everyone."

"Take your hand off my shoulder," answered Manuel.

"You've got to try to keep your head above water. Learn to play the flute or the guitar."

"Take your damn hand off my shoulder," Manuel gasped. "I don't need anyone's hand on my shoulder. And I don't need any good advice!"

Uncle Lazaro worked in the harbor at Coquimbo until just before Christmas, then his fellows, the stevedores, took him on a pilgrimage to Andacollo. The footpath snaked up into the barren clay mountains. After two days they reached the high plateau. In its middle lay Andacollo, the city of the Mother of God. Above its roofs towered the cathedral.

It had been built of wood, for though there was plenty of stone around Andacollo, the Madonna had to have something rare, something special, not a stone cathedral, like those in every other city. And so the worshippers of the Mother of God had sent for wood from California, and now it stood there, the huge wooden cathedral, before the little Uncle Lazaro from Marga-Marga.

The place was seething with pilgrims. Lazaro looked with awe at the Madonna, crawled on his knees through the cathedral up to the altar, commended to her his family, his home town, and even the little Indian girl from the oasis of Calama, and lighted several candles for them.

"Just as you like," the corporal replied and withdrew his hand. "I only mean well toward you, I only want to help you. Seriously, you ought to learn how to play some instrument, then you can earn money and get something to eat, and without offending anybody."

Manuel's mind could not grasp this advice. His ears did not even hear it. He was only waiting for an answer to his question and now he repeated it: "So you don't think I could strangle someone?"

"If you have to feel for his throat first, he'll be faster than you, I'm afraid."

Manuel moved closer to the corporal, who was now leaning against the wall with his eyes closed.

"So you don't think I'm up to it?"

"Don't be silly."

"Yes or no?"

"If you absolutely must have an answer—no."

At that, Manuel leaped to his feet and hurled himself at the corporal. Searching for his throat, he hit the man's face with outspread fingers and one of them struck his eye. The corporal was unprepared for the attack, he fell sideways and held his hand to his eye, which was beginning to stream.

"No more jokes, Manuel," he said. "You've poked me in the eye!"

He tried to fend him off with his other hand.

"Watch out, I'm ticklish," he said.

Manuel groped. Where was his throat?

"What are you doing?" shouted the corporal. "Are you drunk? You're tickling me!"

But Manuel was beside himself with rage. He threw himself full length on top of the corporal and now he found his throat. The people sitting near the fire got up to see what was happening. Visitors emerging from the cemetery on their way home came over to the fire and asked what was going on. A woman screamed, but was quickly hushed; there was a gendarme involved here, it was better to be quiet. But her little boy tugged at her hand, he wanted to run to Manuel.

"Just stay here!" she cried softly. "This is something you don't want to get mixed up in!"

"But that's the man whose eyes flew away!" the boy cried in excitement.

Manuel had both hands around the corporal's neck. The corporal took his hand from his eyes, surged to his feet and struck out. Manuel did not let go. Then the corporal hit him in the stomach with his fist.

Manuel screamed, fell on his side and doubled up with pain.

"And I know why he jumped on him. That man took his eyes away!" the boy cried.

"Be still," commanded his mother. "What do you know about it? You'll make the corporal angry with your nonsense."

She dragged him away, but the youngster turned around and kept staring at the corporal's face. So that's what the eyes looked like, the eyes that had been stolen from his friend. And the gendarme wouldn't give them back!

"The corporal is a pig!" the boy shouted.

"Holy Mother of God!" his mother said and struck him in the mouth so hard that tears shot from his eyes.

It was wonderful here, Lazaro decided to stay. Even some Bolivian pilgrims who had come down from Oruro could not persuade him to return home. He remained in that wretched mountain town of Andacollo, which came to life only once a year, between Christmas and New Year's, and the rest of the time roasted, dust-covered and dead, in the sun between the yellow hills. He remained to increase the number of the unemployed until a few months later gold fever broke out on the hillsides around the town.

This was not the first time. There had been other gold strikes in Andacollo. They always ran out, and at the time of Lazaro's arrival there was nothing to remind one of the strikes except a few stone crushers. But now the gold diggers came swarming in hordes over the hills to dig in the sands around Andacollo. They created a lunar landscape, digging their way from the outskirts into the town itself. They undermined everything, even the Californian cathedral. Andacollo became a boom town. There were fights and killings. The few stores in the place blossomed overnight. This many people had never come for the Mother of God festival!

And Lazaro caught on quickly. He stole a spade and joined the digging. The Madonna was gracious to him, she arranged for him to dig in a spot that proved to be one of the best. He sold the gold to itinerant dealers and a year later was a rich man.

The corporal knelt down beside Manuel and bent over him.

"Listen to me," he said. "I didn't like doing that, but what choice had I? I couldn't breathe. You know I'm willing to close one eye as far as you're concerned—you deserve that—but I'm on duty now, we can't rough-house here. Go home and sleep it off. Your head's full of candle fumes and new wine."

The people stood and stared. What would Manuel do now? The corporal had hit him and rebuked him. He didn't have much choice but to disappear as fast as possible. And that's what he did. He got up groaning and staggered out of the firelight without saying another word.

"Poor devil," said the corporal, seating himself again comfortably beside the fire once more.

He said it softly, but Manuel heard it.

The people dispersed. There was nothing more to see. Don Eugenio strolled by. The corporal saw only his silhouette beyond the fire, but he recognized the voice that said: "Any news, corporal?"

The gendarme sprang to his feet and saluted.

"All quiet, captain."

Don Eugenio nodded and went on. The corporal stood for a while stiff as a post, staring after Don Eugenio. Then he sat down beside the fire again, but alert and ready to spring to his feet at any moment. The captain might return. Who knew what he was up to?

His aunt's dying, thought the corporal. Why doesn't he go home? We'll make out all right here without him. But that's the way he is, he wants to be on the scene all the time. A strange sort of captain. The one we had before didn't give a damn about anything; he let All Souls' Day run its natural course.

Now he was seized with a longing for Bolivia. He sewed his money into his jacket, took a tearful farewell of the Madonna and, descending into the lowland, bought a railroad ticket. He began by going astray twice and then succeeded in reaching Uyoni by way of the oasis of Calama; from there he went to Oruro. In a small dive in Oruro where he planned to while away the evening, before catching a morning freight train that would take him home, he told about his good luck, happy to be among Bolivians again and no longer so far from Marga-Marga. His drinking companions found the story believable. They applauded his plans: he planned to buy the largest house in Marga-Marga. They got him drunk, took his jacket and disappeared.

A few days later he arrived home in a state of perfect equanimity, once more on foot. It simply was not to be. Even without a fortune he was boisterously welcomed. No one had believed he would ever return.

From then on he stayed at home, let his children look after him, and told all who would listen about his adventures in foreign lands, and he never omitted the little Indian girl. And if one asked about the theft of his money, he would say, smiling: "May they enjoy it under the protection of the Madonna!"

A few months later he died, still not very old, and was buried in the cemetery of Marga-Marga. And now they had all come out to visit him: his wife, his daughters and sons, his brother, his nieces and nephews. And the bride, his niece, had sat down on his grave together with her bridegroom.

"Believe me, the world is full of mysteries, but everything depends on whether the Madonna is with you, he always said," giggled the aunt. "He was my husband. He was a great man! He was on familiar terms with the Madonna!"

The women brought out dried meat, bread, and fruit.

"Eat, people," the bridegroom's father said. "The night is long."

There were smackings and slurpings on Uncle Lazaro's grave. The jugs wandered from mouth to mouth, the guests drank and nodded to one another; the wine was good, nothing had been spared. Here and there someone began to laugh. Yes, yes, it was a wonderful night!

The musicians at the fountain and at the crossing of the paths had stopped playing, the dancing was ended, but now many voices rose, spreading a wild medley of song through the cemetery. A light breeze blew across the graves, making the lights flicker, and wafting the noises over the square of the cemetery all the way out to the gate, where the hawkers stood half asleep behind their tables.

"The dogs," said the bride. "They're back again."

"My Lazaro!" the aunt cried. "If he were alive today, then none of this would have happened!"

"What happened?" asked the mother.

"That young man wouldn't have been strangled!"

"Be quiet!" cried the younger brother of the bride.

But the aunt didn't listen to him; she shouted out her thoughts.

"My Lazaro would have separated the two," she went on. "He would have torn Manuel's hands from the drummer's throat and beaten him to a pulp!"

"Will you shut your mouth!" said the bride's older brother and shook her.

"He was a big man, he was a strong man!" she screamed.

"Nonsense," said the older brother. "Uncle Lazaro was a small man with thin muscles. I was bigger than him when I was fourteen. Don't you remember? Even you were bigger than him."

"That's not true!" howled the aunt. "He was a big man."

"He had traveled far and knew a lot," the younger brother said, "but he didn't grow any bigger because of that. He was little when he left and little when he came back."

"Yes, yes, he was little," the aunt sobbed. "He was little and he was no good. He came home poor and brought nothing for me, not even a little madonna!"

She stood up and began to shake the cross on Uncle Lazaro's grave.

"Damn you, Lazaro!" she shrieked. "Couldn't you have taken better care of the money? Today I'd be living in the big house on the plaza, I could be sitting on the balcony right now, between the blue pillars, and sewing!"

The bride's two brothers drew her down and began to reason with her, but she tore herself away from them and closed her ears. With both fists she beat on the grave and howled.

"You'll anger him yet," said the bridegroom's mother in alarm. "And who knows what he'll do to us then? Don't forget that he's dead."

The aunt's howls turned to shrill laughter.

"Nobody could make him angry," she shouted. "He is too good! He's so good nobody can stand him!"

"Forgive her," whispered the mother. "You can see that she's drunk."

The bride's little sister was hurrying through the cemetery. She could not find Manuel anywhere; she would have been content to just catch a glimpse of his figure, but he was neither at the wall nor between the graves, nor was he leaning against the fountain. She passed the drum, still lying where it had rolled. No one had noticed it, no one had picked it up and taken it to the gendarmes. The little one pushed it aside with her foot. She went on, but after a few steps she returned and threw her poncho over it. She slipped up to the gate and peered out. There was the fire, there sat the gendarme, staring motionless into the flames. People were squatting on the far side of the fire and warming themselves. Manuel was not among them.

She felt cold as she hurried back to the wedding party.

"Where's your poncho?" asked the bride.

"Over the drum."

"And where's the drum?" asked the groom's father.

"Under the poncho."

"Now I know exactly," said the groom's father. "Stop your nonsense, girl, and tell me where the drum is."

"I threw my poncho over it," the little one answered. "And now no one will see it."

She curled up next to the bride.

"Stubborn creature," said the groom's father. "Make her talk, you're her sister."

"She doesn't know," said the bride. "The cemetery is big. She got frightened and ran away. Let her sleep."

"But the drum!"

"Let her sleep," said the older brother. "The drum is hidden, no one will take it during the night. Tomorrow when it's light the bridegroom can find it. It isn't heavy, he can bring it with him to Marga-Marga and give it to you before he leaves."

"Just the same, we ought to go and look for it," said the groom's father.

"Now we're here with Lazaro," the aunt cried, "and here we stay. Why should we be afraid? We didn't strangle the boy. Manuel should hide the drum himself. And even if they caught him with it they wouldn't believe him!"

So they stayed where they were, on Uncle Lazaro's grave, and left the drum where it was. They had done what they could, and the groom could take care of the drum the next morning. They drank in honor of Uncle Lazaro, and although horror still lingered in their bones, they knew what they owed to that famous uncle.

"Drink, people," the father said. "There's plenty here."

The shadows between the lights belched. Yes, the drummer was dead, but this was All Souls' Day, and there had been a wedding—reason for joy! And laughter swelled up over the grave. The two musicians had drunk a lot, the flute player's head was wobbling. The bride suddenly threw her head back and laughed. The wine had made her bridegroom merry too. He sprang to his feet.

"Now tell me what I should bring you from the Gran Chaco when I come back," he shouted, looking around the circle.

"A gold watch," called the guitarist.

"A bottle of brandy," said an old man.

"A petticoat of flowered silk," a girl said, tittering with embarrassment.

The bride's little sister slept a restless sleep. She kept hearing her aunt's harsh voice. Under the poncho her sister had spread over her she kept twisting and turning.

"Just let her sleep," said the older of the two brothers. "She was terribly upset."

The younger brother drove away the dogs that had begun to sniff at her.

The drummer was sitting on Uncle Lazaro's grave, his legs apart, the drum between his knees. He was beating on it with the palms of his hands. The drum rumbled. His face was full of sweat, his ears were big and red, his pockmarks glowed. He threw his head back and sang, and suddenly the girl saw a grave cross behind him begin to move. The wreath on it twitched to the beat. The crosses on neighboring graves also came to life, they swung back and forth like pendulums, the wreaths rolled around their axes. The candles hopped up and vaulted through the wreaths or turned pirouettes in the air. The crosses stamped, the wreaths wheezed, the lights chirped like cicadas. The drummer did not see, he beat the drum with closed eyes. The crosses grew taller out of the earth, they pulled up their wooden lathes from the graves and, staggering in step over the mounds, from the farthest corners of the cemetery, they came stalking, never losing the rhythm of the drum. They bowed and straightened, they swayed to and fro, their wreaths hopped. They formed a circle around the drummer, the little white crosses on the inside, the black ones on the outside, they moved slowly around him to the rhythm of the drum which gradually got faster. The wreaths wheezed louder, they glistened wetly in the light of the whirling candles. The stamping of the crosses quickened, rising and sinking in time, advancing and retreating like the waves of the sea. The young man's hands whirled on the drum, faster, faster, the mounds sharpened into points, the crosses leaped up, the lights collected like gnats around the boy's head, the circle narrowed, with every beat the crosses came closer and closer, and then, as he began the final mad roll of the drum, one of the crosses flew into the air and smashed down upon the boy's head. Another cross, then many crosses, pitched down on him, each dragging its wreath. The boy shrieked, threw his hands in the air, blood ran down his face, but now it was hidden by the wreaths and crosses, and the crosses beat the rhythm on the painted tin under which the drummer lay. The wreaths still jerked and quivered, and the lights above them whirled madly together. The heap on top of the boy rose higher and higher, towered far above the walls of the cemetery, and only when the crosses and wreaths from all the graves were gathered on top of him did the mountain grow quiet, stop quivering and lie still.

"Manuel didn't do it," the girl whispered in her sleep. She ventured up to the heap and pulled at one of the crosses, but it was afire. She burned her fingers. The lights circling above the mound flew off in a wedge like a flight of wild geese. It grew completely dark.

"But it was not Manuel!" the girl murmured.

"What about the rest of you?" cried the bridegroom. "Everyone has a wish. Out with them! I'll bring something for each of you. Down there you can get anything. Yes, sir!"

"A beautiful young wife, a white, from Asunción, with blond hair and pearls in her ears," said the flute player.

Everyone laughed.

"What do you want with a beautiful white wife? You're too old for her. You would bore her."

"She will carry my flute for me," he cackled. "Then it will give a clearer tone."

"She'll not only carry it for you, she'll blow on it too. Then you'll have to dance to her tune!" cried the aunt.

During the laughter the old man raised the jug to his lips and didn't set it down again.

"Don't overdo it," the guitarist said. "You have another wedding tomorrow, you know, in Huapi."

"Tomorrow night, you people," burped the flute player, "tomorrow night—tomorrow night—"

"Now he's forgotten what he had in mind for tomorrow," the bride said.

"Bring me back my great Lazaro, nephew, from the Chaco," the aunt cried. "What am I without him?"

"I'll bring you anything you want," the groom answered.

"I'll come home a general," cried the bride's younger brother, and beat himself on the breast. "I'll have as much to tell as Uncle Lazaro when he got back."

Tears were streaming down the older brother's face. He hid it in his hands.

"And you, what shall I bring you?" the groom asked the bride.

She sprang to her feet, raised her arms and laughed. "A bouquet of flowers."

He knew it would probably take him two or three weeks traveling to get back from the Chaco. How would he keep a bouquet fresh for that long? But the wine made everything so simple, even the long trip with the flowers, even the war. Everything would turn out right, and he would hand his bride the flowers, as fresh as if they had just been picked.

"I'll bring back even more," he said in a loud voice. "I'll come home with boxes and chests, I'll capture a Guarani and make him carry my luggage. Then things will be better for everyone, and then we two will live in the great house in Marga-Marga, and will be able to hire twelve musicians when we want music. We'll buy the mines, all the mines around here, all of them! We'll be richer than the uncle ever was. I'll always wear a jacket, I'll—"

He could not think of anything else. He sat on the ground again and went on drinking.

"You'll hear and see a great many things in the Chaco," his father said. "But even so don't forget to send us news of how you are. Don't forget you have families at home."

"We can't write, father," the groom replied.

"You'll surely be able to find someone who can write a letter for you."

"Yes, there's sure to be someone among the troops who can put a few letters together," his mother said. "It doesn't need to be much. Only a few words, just so we know you're all right."

"And I'll tell you one thing," cried the groom, springing up again. "When I come home I'll have a grave built for the drummer in the rich people's cemetery, a splendid grave with Christ on the cross and angels, like on the grave of the Mayor's mother!"

"Do you hear me?" whispered his mother. "Don't forget to write. We'll go to the priest and have him read your letter to us."

"It will be the finest grave in the cemetery, and everyone will ask who lies there."

"Even if it's only a few words, just so we'll know you're still alive . . ."

"His mother will be proud of him because he has such a splendid grave. It will be so big that there will be room for her in it too. I won't count the cost."

"You need only to pray enough for us," said the bride's older brother.

"We're all going straight to paradise," the flute player shouted hoarsely. "Just keep drinking until we're all there together, along with the drummer and Manuel."

The bride's father returned to the cemetery across the moon-blue plain. Its lights shone far off. Pedro had stayed at home with his donkey. Everything had gone well. The drummer's mother was probably still sitting in the corner where he had found her, weeping quietly to herself. But she had promised not to denounce Manuel.

I don't think any of us would denounce him, he thought. It would be a shameful thing to do.

Pedro's wife and her sister would look after the drummer's mother tomorrow. She would slowly allow herself to be comforted, and after all she still had a married daughter. Oh, God, the old woman hadn't even screamed when he had told her, but when he rolled the poncho from the boy she had grown very pale. And then she had taken him on her lap and rocked him, and only then had she begun to weep.

Lanterns were glowing in the dealers' tents and on their tables. He saw the corporal sitting near the fire and smoking. Where is Manuel? he wondered. Before many nights are over, he'll hear the rattling of hell's chains.

He was thirsty and dead tired from the long road that

lay behind him. He could think only of a place beside his sons and of streams of wine: drink and rest for an hour, probably not more than that, for it was getting on for midnight, and then he would have to get up again and make his way home to Marga-Marga. The path up the hillside stretched in front of him, the field of lights on either side swam before his eyes. Far off glittered Emilio's grave. Now it had grown quieter among the graves. People were gathered in small groups, and whoever wasn't drinking was asleep. Well apart from the main circle of drinkers sat his people. Slowly he climbed up to them and let himself sink among them. The laughter subsided. He reached for the jug which the bride was holding out to him.

"Everything go well?" the brothers asked.

"His mother will say it was an accident," the father answered, and after a pause he asked: "What about the eyeglasses? They belong to Don Leo."

"We took them back to him," said his younger son. "We told him we had found them. He had already missed them. He thought the drummer had stolen them and then thrown them away because he was afraid someone might recognize them."

"And the button? Did you give it to her?" the flute player asked.

"Yes, I gave it to her."

Now it grew very quiet on the grave. The only sound was the snoring of the crazy girl. What else was there to say? It had all been said. The wedding party let their heads droop.

"Never have we had such a splendid All Souls' night," the bride whispered and looked up at the sky. A huge halo around the moon covered almost half of it. "Do you remember last year? There was such a storm that none of the candles would stay lit. And the year before there was frost in the cemetery."

"Yes, a good wedding night," said the bridegroom.

The mother of the man who had fallen in action was standing in the darkness outside the wall as Manuel slowly groped his way up the hillside. "You there, since you happen to be passing by, tell me again how it happened."

"Has it gotten around already?" Manuel cried. "Are you torn with curiosity? Why don't you ask those who were there? After all I didn't see it, I just did it."

"What are you talking about?" the woman asked. "Aren't you Manuel?"

"And who are you?"

"Juan's mother."

"Juan's mother? Ah."

"I have put up an altar to the dead for him. Come here and sit down."

"Leave me alone," Manuel answered. "I already told you about it when I first came home. What more do you want to hear? You already know everything."

"Just once more. I still can't believe it. Maybe you were mistaken? Perhaps it wasn't him at all? You were there! Try to remember!"

"Damn it, leave me alone!"

She ran up to him, grabbed his arm and shook him.

"Did you see that it was him?"

"Let me go," Manuel shouted angrily.

"Did you know him at all, you?"

"You know very well that we were friends."

"I can't think of anything but him," she wailed. "His clothes are still hanging in the house, I brush his poncho every Sunday after mass, he was my only child. If he had only come home blind! I would have led him and cared for him! But this way—who can take care of a dead man? Talk to me about him."

"You already know everything that I know," Manuel said. "Let me go. There's no more to tell."

"But you still haven't told me what it looked like, there where it happened."

"What do you think it looked like? Bushes and trees, like everywhere."

"And no grass?"

"No."

"You said he fell on his face. So he must have fallen on his face on the bare ground?"

"He fell on an ammunition chest."

"An iron one?"

She looked at him with horrified eyes.

"He didn't know the difference," he said. "It was all over with him immediately. I've told you that before. I said 'Juan!' to him, but he couldn't hear me."

"Perhaps he was only unconscious?"

"No, he was dead. But if you must know: it caught him in the middle of a joke. We saw two birds flying by, yellow birds with long blue tails, one behind the other, and the air was all blue. Then he said: 'Do you know the story about the bridal pair on the way to the church?'— 'No,' we said. He began to laugh even before he had told it. That's when it happened."

200 |

"I know the joke," the woman said. "It's a rather dirty joke."

"Then it belonged down there. And you see, he was laughing when he died. What more do you want? Let me go."

"Tell me one more thing," she cried and ran after him. "How did his face look? Was it contorted? Did he know what happened?"

"It's a good thing you didn't see it."

"No!" she cried. "You're lying!"

Manuel stopped and turned toward her. "All right. As you wish. He looked like an angel. He was smiling as though he had seen heaven. Perhaps he had seen the Madonna, or even you."

"That's all I wanted to know," the woman said and burst into tears. "That's all. He saw me. Now I know everything."

She turned back to her altar to the dead and said no more to Manuel, who slowly began climbing uphill.

The wedding party was listening to the noise of the drinkers on the other mounds. The dogs had curled up and were sleeping among the crosses in the moonlight. Pairs of lovers had withdrawn into the shadow of the wall.

"We don't celebrate a wedding every day," shouted the bride's father, so loud that the guests jumped. "Drink! It will be a long time before my second daughter is married."

He embraced the bride. "Happiness in your new life! Riches and many sons!"

He slapped the groom on the shoulder and said: "Keep her in check, then she will be obedient and true to you."

"Don't look at other men while he's away," said the groom's father. "Until he returns you will live with us and we will look after you."

"And, bride, if you cry I'll stick my head in your window and play for you," said the flute player.

"And if you can't find a godfather for your first son, then just come to me," said the guitarist.

"Long live the bride and groom!" shouted the bride's two brothers. Everyone joined in. They made so much noise on Uncle Lazaro's grave that the other drinkers in the cemetery turned their heads to look. The flute player rolled off the mound and fell asleep.

"It's time for us to go home," said the bridegroom's father. "Will you stay here or come with us?"

"We'll stay here," answered the groom.

"You have to leave just after sunrise. At sunrise we'll be waiting near the busses at the plaza. We'll meet you there, your mother and I, and say goodby."

Shall I hang it around his neck now or tomorrow morning? the mother thought.

"But don't forget to leave here in time, for the army doesn't understand jokes."

"I'll be on time, father."

"Up, people," said the groom's father and got to his feet. "The children are already asleep and we have a long way to go. Besides, the bridal pair has a lot to do before morning."

The groom laughed in embarrassment and stole a

glance at his bride. But her face was in shadow. The women got up heavily, straightened their hats, shook out their skirts. They helped one another tie the children to their backs and help the swaying men to their feet. The bride woke her little sister.

"It's time. The others are going home," she whispered.

"Shall I stay with you?" the girl whispered back.

"Just go," the bride said, "tomorrow morning I'll come and tell you all about it."

"Aren't you afraid?"

"Yes, I am."

"I could protect you."

The bride shook her head.

The little one stood up and wrapped herself in the poncho.

"Was I asleep?" she asked.

"Yes, sound asleep."

"Do you really think I should go home?"

"What else?"

"All right, then I'll go."

"Only don't worry about me," the bride said.

"No," the little one answered.

She took a few steps, then turned around again and whispered: "Was Manuel here while I was asleep? Did you see him?"

"He wasn't here, and I haven't seen him."

"He's nowhere. He isn't anywhere in the whole cemetery."

"Why do you want to know where he is? Let him go where he likes! Stay away from him, he is nothing but trouble. He is a puma, he tears to pieces whatever he gets hold of."

"What do you know about him?" the girl exclaimed. "Maybe you know more about him than we do?"

"I guess not," the girl said softly.

"He doesn't want you. He doesn't want anyone. Didn't you notice how he looks down on all of us? We're dust under his feet. Go home with the others and don't think of him any more. He'll get along. He is a man. He won't give up easily."

The girl let her head droop and slipped away.

"Where are you going?" the younger brother called after her.

"Home," she answered, without turning around.

"Why don't you wait for us? We're all going home now."

"I'll go on ahead. You'll catch up with me."

"You'll get scared, all alone."

"The moon is shining."

The flute player and the guitarist were still asleep. No one had been able to wake them, although their heads lay in the ditch between the graves and their legs up on the mound. The mad girl's father carried her in his arms, for she had not wanted to leave Uncle Lazaro's grave and refused to walk. It was a small crowd, it walked down the middle path with bent backs, sleepy eyes, weary feet. Children sighed in their sleep. The jugs clanged hollowly as they banged together in the baskets and bundles.

"Goodby, daughter," said the bride's father, standing awkwardly before her and looking down at her hands which toyed self-consciously with a ribbon on her blouse. Nor did she look at him, but stared at her toes.

"Goodby," she said.

"He will be kind to you, he's a good boy. Enjoy this night, you will have to wait a long time for the next one. And don't be surprised. Whatever happens will be the way it should be."

"Yes, Father."

He stroked her gently on the arm.

The mother was the last one to leave the bridal pair.

"I have something more for you, my son," she whispered. "But I'm not going to give it to you until tomorrow morning, before you leave. I will see you tomorrow morning, won't I?"

"For sure, Mother."

"It's something very important."

The bride's father shouted up from the fountain: "Have you seen the little one?"

"She's gone on ahead," the bride called back.

The bridal party had gathered around the basin and were drinking.

"I have to go now," the mother whispered. "But we will see each other again tomorrow, won't we?"

"Yes, Mother."

She walked a few steps away and turned around again: "It's quite certain that I will see you tomorrow morning?"

"I'll be at the plaza by sunrise, Mother. You know that."

She nodded tenderly to him once more, and then trotted after the others. She was weighed down by the jugs and the basket and the bundle on her back. She kept looking back as the procession left the fountain and staggered along the path between the lights on the graves toward the gate.

THE BRIDE'S LITTLE SISTER WANDERED BY THE GEN-
darme's fire. Manuel was not there.

"Have you seen Manuel?" she asked a woman who
was crouching on the ground not far from the fire, with
her sleeping children beside her.

"Who is Manuel?" the woman asked sullenly. "I don't
live here. I'm from San Pablo. I can't know everybody in
the cemetery."

"He's blind."

"The one with the frightful face? He was here. He
tried to start a fight with the corporal, but the corporal
gave it to him. I saw it. One blow in the belly and it was
all over."

"Where is he now?" the girl asked.

"Who knows? He went away."

"Didn't you see where he went?"

"Over there, along the wall. It's so dark—who could
tell where he was going? Why should I care? The corporal was friendly. The one with the face started the fight.
What an idiot—to pick a fight with a gendarme!"

The girl went to look for Manuel. She left the area of the booths and tents and lanterns and went along the outside of the wall, which lay in moonlight. Here the only lights were the candles burning on the altars to the dead. If Manuel was still around, he must be somewhere along the wall and it could not be hard to find him, for there was almost no one left outside the cemetery. The dead had been cared for. Even old Louisa had long since struck her tent. Anyone who had not left for home had gone back inside the cemetery or had drawn near the gate, for here, outside the wall, it was eerie. Here there were the stray dogs and the straying dead. The bride's small sister knew that. She was very frightened as she began to climb the slope, but what else could she do if she wanted to find Manuel?

She found him above the cemetery. He was leaning against the wall not far from where Louisa's tent had stood. She stopped beside him.

"Is that you, corporal?" Manuel asked after a while.

"No, it's me," the girl answered in her childish voice.

"So you're back again, you daughter of a whore," Manuel said. "You stick to my heels. Didn't I tell you to leave me in peace?"

The little one didn't answer.

"I don't need you. Disappear."

The girl crouched down, she was trembling, but she did not go away.

"What do you want from me?" he shouted angrily.

"To stay with you," she whispered.

He leaned against the wall and did not move. The girl stared up at him, she saw his tall figure looming before her. His shadow fell on her.

"Look at my face," he said. "Is the moon shining on it?"

"Yes."

"Doesn't it scare you?"

"No."

Suddenly he pushed himself from the wall with a violent motion and felt for her.

"Here I am," she said, creeping toward him.

He seized her meager arm, pulled her to her feet and pressed her to himself. But in the next moment he let her go and pushed her away. She stumbled and fell backward, and as she lay there on the ground she was so terrified that she did not dare get up.

"What should I do with you, you little monster?" Manuel said. "You're not good for anything."

"I can knit," she sobbed.

"Knit? That's it, that's what I need," he said. "Knit me a rope, then I'll hang myself."

"You want a rope?" she asked breathlessly. "Wait here, I'll be right back."

She sprang up and ran off.

The mother had caught up with the wedding party, but she left it again at the corner of the cemetery wall to run up the slope to the altar for the dead. The jug was upset, the wine had spilled out and run into the sand, the dishes were empty. The dogs had been busy around the altar and had gobbled the food meant for the dead. Only the candles still burned. She packed tarpaulin, grave cross, and dishes in her basket, crossed herself and hurried after the others who were already far out in the plain.

Who knows, she thought, perhaps it was the dead.

And even if it was the dogs, the dead did see that it was put there for them. For the dead see everything that happens in the cemetery. They sit on the wall and wait for us on All Souls' Day, and their eyes are everywhere. Nothing is hidden from them. My little ones had no paltry altar, they needn't feel ashamed. Your mother looks out for you, you must admit that, children, even on your brother's wedding day.

The girl ran along the wall to the booths. But only a few dealers were there now, and none of them had a rope he was willing to give away.

"Have you any money?" asked Don Leo.

"No."

"And what do you need a rope for so late at night?"

"Manuel wants it."

"Go home to your family. If Manuel needs a rope let him get it for himself."

"But he can't see anything!"

"Then what does he need a rope for?"

"He wants to hang himself."

"If you're making fun of me, I'll knock you down," said Don Leo. "I've had enough trouble for one day."

"I never give anything away," said the fat candle dealer from Merengue.

"I haven't any rope with me," said the woman who sold cakes. "I brought everything here in baskets. Go home, it's already past midnight. Your parents will beat you for wandering around alone so late at night."

The girl came across a donkey tied to the leg of a table. She looked around cautiously. There was no one around. Here was her chance. She unknotted the rope from the donkey's bridle and worked the noose down under the bottom of the table leg. The rope was still good. Manuel would be happy.

"Not here," the groom said to the bride when they were alone. "I know a better place."

"With one of your dead?"

"Neither with our dead nor with yours. There's a place that people seldom visit."

He took her by the hand and drew her away.

"I'm tired," she said.

"Now's the time to wake up. We only have a few hours left."

She let him lead her along, but then she pulled free and ran off between the graves. He called. She laughed. He tried to catch her. She flitted here and there on all the many paths, she doubled in her tracks and hid, she rattled tin wreaths behind his back. She screamed like a screech-owl between the plaster angels of the rich. She let him come near and then disappeared again.

"Stand still, you!" he shouted breathlessly.

She clucked her tongue. Where was she? Was she lying in a furrow beside a grave? Was she crouching behind a cross peeping through a tin wreath? Was she huddled behind the fountain? He turned around and around, staring at the moonlight and the shadows, until suddenly her hands closed over his eyes from behind.

"Now I've got you!" the groom cried, whirling around and seizing her by the braids. She thrust her elbows against his breast and tried to get free.

"Let me go," she said. "You're hurting me!"

"You've lost your hat."

Arms around each other, they went to look for the hat, but could not find it.

"I'll bring you another from Paraguay," he whispered. "We'll not look for it any more now."

"But it's a new one," she replied, distressed.

"The one from Paraguay will be much prettier."

They hurried up the middle path, then around the fountain, in which the moon sparkled, and sprinkled themselves with water. Their faces gleamed wet.

"I want a drink," said the bride.

She bent her head to the pipe, but he pushed her away, caught the water in his hands, and offered it to her.

"Are you afraid?"

"Yes."

He laughed softly. Then he drew her with him up to Emilio's grave.

"Look at the flowers," the bride cried. "Even lilies. Do you see them? The moon's shining on them."

"Come now," the groom said.

They went on straight across the field of crosses. A few people, stumbling wearily toward the gate, turned to look at them.

"Who were those two?" a woman asked.

"The bridegroom and the bride," another answered.

"He must be off to the Chaco tomorrow morning," a man said. "They're right; they should have their fling, who knows how soon she'll be a widow."

The groom led his bride into one of the upper corners of the cemetery. Here there was plenty of room left for the future dead. Stiff, sparse grass grew here. In this corner no one was drinking, no one was asleep, for the people were frightened of the place. Only a dog leaped up and ran away. A single grave lay in the shadow of the wall.

"Beside the woman who committed suicide?" the bride asked in dismay.

"Why, we can stay a little way away," the groom replied.

They settled down in the shadow of the wall. He spread out his poncho and lay down on it. She knelt beside him.

"Tomorrow morning you must leave," she said.

"Forget it," he replied.

She pulled at a strand of black hair that fell across his eyes.

"How many sons do you want to have?" she asked.

"Five."

"And what shall we call them?"

"The first for my father," he said and stroked her face.

"And the second for mine."

"The third for my grandfather."

"The fourth must be Lazaro."

"The fifth for my oldest brother, the one who died."

"But which will have your name?"

"Five won't be enough," he whispered. "We must have more. One must also be named Simon, for Bolivar, and I wanted to name one after the President."

"But don't we want to have a few daughters too?" the bride asked.

"If only we can manage all that."

"But we have years and years, a whole lifetime."

"Come here, come here," he whispered, "it's only a few hours until I have to leave, oh, you! I have never called you Gorina—"

She bent over him. "Then say it now," she whispered.

"Gorina."

"You have a pretty name too. I can write it!"

"You can write Pablo?" he asked incredulously.

She nodded proudly. "I've been practicing it for a long time, but it isn't really so hard. You can read it too; I showed it to a man who can read and he recognized at once that it said Pablo."

"In the Chaco I'll get them to show me how to write Gorina."

"They'll tease you."

"Oh, Gorina!"

But Manuel was no longer in his old place. The little girl ran back and forth beside the upper wall, looked behind a pile of stones and peered over the ridge of the hill. She ran behind the wall, which led downhill on the other side of the cemetery, and there she finally found him. He was huddled between two of the altars to the dead.

"Here's your rope," she cried.

He didn't answer.

"Manuel, your rope!" she cried again and laid it in his hands.

"What kind of rope?" he asked, feeling it.

"Didn't you want a rope?"

"Have you brought a tree too? What am I supposed to hang myself from in this cemetery where there's nothing but stones and walls?"

"Then you aren't going to hang yourself?" the girl asked happily.

"How can I, you bitch? When I want to hang myself,

there's no tree. When I want to drown myself, there's no water. I can't shoot myself because I have no pistol. I must live, whether I want to or not. Now you know."

"Why don't you want to live?"

"What's that to you? I'm frightened."

"What are you frightened of?"

"Oh, hell, why do you pester me? Go where you like but leave me in peace. I'm going home now, but without you and your whining."

"How will you find your way?" the girl asked. "Marga-Marga is all quiet now, you couldn't even find it with your ears. You'll just wander off somewhere. You need someone to lead you. If you like, I'll lead you, because I'm going home now too."

"I don't need you or anybody else to lead me!" he roared and, throwing the rope away, groped past the altars to the dead, down the hillside. The girl picked up the rope and he heard her steps as she followed him. He turned around and threatened her with his fist. She stopped for a while, then followed him as quietly as she could. He was trying to find his way through the tents and booths. From a distance she saw that he was getting farther and farther from the wall. He stumbled straight out into the plain, but not in the direction of Marga-Marga, in a direction where there was no village. The girl ran and caught up with him. Softly she said: "You're going the wrong way, Manuel. Marga-Marga isn't that way. You must turn around and go back."

"How would you know where I want to go?" Manuel answered angrily.

But he turned around and walked toward the cemetery and arrived almost exactly at the gate. The girl trotted after him. Just in front of the wall Don Leo stepped in her path and seized her by the arm.

"Show me, what have you there?" he asked. "Isn't that a rope? So you're the one who stole my rope, you brat! You untied my donkey! I was just coming to get it and ride home, but it was gone, it was half a mile out on the plain and grazing! What were you planning to do? Jump rope, eh? Give it to me, you slut!"

He tore the rope out of her hands and hit her over the head with it. She ducked and whimpered softly, then she ran away.

Manuel had walked ahead, ignoring her. He had gone past the cemetery gate and was feeling his way along the wall, toward the fire.

"You're going wrong again," the little one said. "Marga-Marga isn't that way either. You're going toward the gendarme who is sitting by the fire."

"Is it the corporal?" Manuel asked.

"No, the other one."

"That's good."

"But Marga-Marga is behind you!" the girl cried. "Turn around, you'll step in the fire!"

Manuel did not turn around. He felt the warmth of the fire on his face and stopped close by it.

"Well, Manuel," said the gendarme, grinning. "Perhaps you would like to report another strangling?"

"I'd like to keep you company at the fire," Manuel answered, "if you're not afraid of me."

"Why should I be afraid of you? Sit down and keep watch with me. The corporal is in the cemetery. Come here and settle yourself."

He stretched out his hand and tried to draw Manuel down, and almost lost his balance in the process.

"Here is a stone as good as a throne," he said.

"I'd rather sit on your other side," Manuel replied.

"Why? As good as a throne, I say. There's even a sheepskin on it, as you can see."

He broke off and began to laugh at his own words.

"Dear God, as though you could see!" he shouted.

"I'd rather sit on your other side," Manuel repeated.

The gendarme stopped laughing and gawked stupidly at Manuel.

"A habit from the war," Manuel said. "I like to have my right side free."

"As you like," said the gendarme. "Anyone who lost both eyes in the war has a right to his preferences."

Manuel did not answer. The gendarme changed places with him. His wine-heavy breath blew in Manuel's face.

"A blessed night," the gendarme said. "What a fiesta! It does something for you."

Manuel was silent.

"You certainly made us hold our breath with your story . . ."

Manuel did not stir. He had leaned his head against the wall and drawn his legs up.

"What ideas you have," the gendarme went on. "But right now, you're not very talkative."

There was no answer.

"Hey, are you asleep?"

He threw a pitying look at Manuel. Such a handsome fellow. The firelight flickered on his ruined face.

A half hour more and I'll be relieved, he thought. The

fire's out here, but inside you can get something to drink. Who will notice if I let a glass be forced on me? The captain is still there, he's wandering around in the cemetery and talking to people, but today he sees nothing, for he isn't in uniform. The devil only knows why he doesn't go home.

"Hey," he said to the bride's little sister, who was huddled on the opposite side of the fire, "what are you doing here again? Go on home, your parents will be looking for you."

The girl shook her head, but pulled back into the darkness. The gendarme's eyes closed. He propped his elbows on his knees and rested his chin in his hands. After a while the bride's little sister came out of the darkness once more and squatted beside the fire. She was watching Manuel. She saw that he was not asleep, she noticed that he was edging closer to the gendarme and groping for him very cautiously. Her mouth fell open, her eyes were wide. The gendarme began to snore. Manuel touched his pistol holster with his fingertips, bent over it and opened it.

The gendarme gave a sudden start and opened his eyes.

"Who's there?" he called.

"No one, no one," Manuel answered softly. "Just sleep, I'll keep watch. If anyone wants you I'll wake you up."

He did not move until the gendarme had fallen asleep again. Then he went to work on the holster again, which was now open. He was familiar with these holsters and also with the pistols they held. The girl watched him as he carefully drew the weapon out, breathless, she looked on as he ran both hands over the pistol, slid back the safety catch and raised the weapon to his face. He pressed the muzzle into one of his eye sockets. The girl bent far forward and pressed her fists into her mouth. The gendarme groaned in his sleep, and Manuel fired. His hands let the pistol fall and slowly dropped, then he slipped sideways from his seat and fell face forward into the ashes that were strewn around the fire.

The gendarme leaped up. Blinded by the glare of the fire, he stared at the girl. She had sprung to her feet and was shrieking, letting out shrill, unchildlike screams. She was not looking at Manuel's body. Her head was thrown back and her eyes were tightly closed.

"Holy Madonna of Copacabana!" shouted the gendarme. "Get the corporal, someone here has shot himself!"

He moved back and put the fire between himself and Manuel.

"O Holy Madonna of Copacabana," he howled. "And he did it with my pistol! He shot himself with my pistol, the scoundrel, just to ruin me!"

He struck his forehead with both fists. Then he rushed at the bride's small sister, seized her by the arm and shook her.

"You saw it, that he took it away from me by force, yes, indeed, by force! As I was sitting peacefully by the fire keeping watch, he forced it away from me!"

The girl continued to scream until one of the people who had come running up slapped her on the ear. Someone ran off to fetch the corporal. By the time he arrived, there was already a dense circle of onlookers around the fire.

"It's not my fault!" the gendarme shouted at the corporal. "He took it away from me by force!"

The corporal bent over Manuel, whose head lay in a pool of blood.

"He's still alive," he said. "We must get a priest."

"A priest, a priest!" several women screamed.

"Take my horse and ride to the parish house in Marga-Marga," the corporal said to a young man. "And hurry if you don't want him to go to hell!"

The fellow's face disappeared from the firelight. More and more of the curious pushed their way into the circle.

"Can you see him, Serafina?" an old woman asked. "Who is it?"

Serafina pushed her way forward. She did not at once recognize Manuel.

"A young man," she said softly to her mother-in-law, who was standing behind her and could see nothing but the glow of the firelight.

"Do you know him?"

"No."

"It's a blind man," someone near her said.

She was startled. Was it Manuel? She looked at his hair.

"It's Manuel," she stammered.

"Who is Manuel? Do you know him?"

Serafina stared at the body beside the fire.

"Answer me, will you? Do you know him?"

"He sometimes came to Don Leo's to buy things. He's from Marga-Marga."

"Strange," said the old woman. "They say he shot

himself. Move a bit to the side, I want to see him myself. To shoot oneself, especially on this night! Can you understand it?"

"No," Serafina cried. "No!"

"Are you crazy? Don't talk so loud. What will people think? Come along, this is nothing for you. We'll go home. It's a long way across the pampa."

Serafina obeyed. She stumbled out of the circle and seized her mother-in-law's arm.

"He has looked horrible since he's been blind," she gasped. "You can't imagine how he looked. Like the living death. When you saw his face you were overcome with terror."

"Don't run so."

"Nothing in his eye sockets, and the lids were gone too. He looked so horrible that everyone looked away. Believe me, you would have been terrified too."

"I've seen a lot. I'm not so easily terrified."

"But even you would have been frightened, I know you would. Everyone was frightened!"

"Why are you rushing so? First you don't want to leave, now you're in a hurry."

"There's nothing one can do if one's terrified by a face like that!" Serafina cried and hurried on. "Either one can stand it or one can't!"

"Well, stop talking about it now. What does it matter to us? He isn't from Merengue."

"No," Serafina repeated softly. "What does it matter to us if he isn't from Merengue."

"It will be windy on the pampa."

"But there's no frost."

"What's that?" said the old woman. "Are you talking about frost? Of course there's no frost, it's November. I guess you're already asleep."

"It gave me the horrors," Serafina murmured, turning around.

"What's the matter? What are you going to do?"

"I'm going back now to look at him once more. I'm going to look him straight in the face."

"You're crazy," the old woman said. "Tomorrow morning you have to go back to Don Leo's, and it's way past midnight now. We spent enough time at the fiesta, and I saw how you strutted past the men and gave them the eye. And not even a year has passed!"

"Why are you pushing so, you devils?" shouted the corporal. "Haven't you ever seen anyone die before?"

He drove the gapers back, but before he had turned around they were there again: pointing, whispering.

Manuel's face lay in the firelight, their eyes probed his wounds, his ghastly face, the two streams of blood trickling over his temple into his hair and down his neck. So this is how someone looked who had shot himself. This was the way mad Manuel looked as he lay dying.

Dogs worked their way through the throng and snuffled at the pool of blood. One of them, a mangy, yellow one, shoved his snout in it and drank greedily. The second gendarme drove him away with a kick in the side.

Manuel no longer heard the snorting of the horse, nor the clatter of his retreating hooves. He also did not feel the corporal spread an empty sack over his head.

"Don Eugenio is coming," people whispered.

The captain strode out of the gate; someone had

informed him. He walked over to Manuel, lifted the sack from his face for an instant and let it fall again. Then he took the two gendarmes aside and talked to them in a quiet voice. The corporal said little, but the other gendarme talked and gesticulated excitedly.

Manuel saw neither him nor the captain, but he saw the monk coming from the lowland. Dry twigs from the Chaco hung in his beard, thorns and burrs stuck to his cowl.

In the field of children's graves the clay horses burst. The wall glowed with phosphorescence. The water in the fountain was burning. A boy with a drum was rushing through the flames that spurted from Emilio's grave. The smoke carried Emilio's flowers high into the air. The monk shot up to the sky, trying to catch the bouquets, but they rose higher and higher. He caught them and gathered them up and threw them over his shoulder into the hood of his cowl until they welled from it in a huge cluster. From the bridal bouquet which he held in his arms rose a storm of white petals. A rainbow-encircled courtyard formed around him. Manuel saw him stamping his feet and dancing, beckoning to him and growing smaller, until he dissolved in blue and moonlight.

The rider was galloping across the plain, chased by his shadow in the moonlight. Halfway to the village he met a man who was running from Marga-Marga toward the cemetery.

"Where are you running to?" the rider shouted at him. "The fiesta is over."

The runner stopped. The fellow on the horse recognized him. He was one of the captain's servants.

"Lend me your horse," he gasped. "I have to fetch Don Eugenio. His aunt is dying. This time she really is dying, perhaps she's already dead. The priest is with her."

"I need the horse myself," the rider answered. "I have to fetch the priest. A man out there has shot himself."

"But the priest is with Señorita Marisol. He won't go with you. Señorita Marisol is Don Eugenio's aunt!"

"I'll try it anyway. It's Manuel," the rider said, gave his horse a blow and rode on. A short distance from the first houses of the town he met the bride's father and her two brothers. They were coming out of the street on their way back to the cemetery. The bride's father stopped the rider.

"Have you seen my daughter? A girl, still a child, very thin—"

"I haven't seen any girl on the way."

"But perhaps at the cemetery?"

"There are a lot of girls there. I don't know them. I'm in a hurry. Let me by."

"No one's stopping you."

When the father and his sons were so far from the town that the silhouettes of the houses were no longer visible against the horizon and the night sky, and the points of light on the graves were just barely discernible, they met a second rider.

"That's Don Eugenio," said the father.

They took off their hats and bowed low as he rode by. None of them dared ask him about the bride's little sister. How could one interrupt his gallop on account of one little girl?

"She will be looking for us," the older brother said.

"She is so frightened she won't dare to walk alone in this dark."

"I'll beat her to a pulp," her father said.

"Another quarter of an hour, we'll be at the gate," said the younger brother.

Behind them rang hoof beats. The rider they had met at the edge of the village was coming back. He galloped by them without greeting them.

There were not many people left around the dead man when the rider reached the cemetery. The two gendarmes were leaning against the wall.

"The priest will come later," he gasped. "He can't leave now. He will take Don Eugenio's horse."

"He'll be too late," said the corporal. "Manuel has been dead for some time. So now he'll go to hell after all, without repentance and extreme unction, and they won't even give him a place in the upper corner of the cemetery. We'll have to take him home to Marga-Marga."

The second gendarme spread out an old tarpaulin. They laid the dead man on it, wrapped him up, carried him to the corporal's horse and lifted him onto it, in front of the saddle. His head dangled, and bloodied the uniform of the second gendarme.

Now the dogs were shameless. In packs they came out of the cemetery, fought over the pool of blood and the torn sack with which the corporal had covered Manuel's face. The corporal pulled a burning stick from the fire and beat them. They tore off howling, but when he got into the saddle they were already back, watching him with distrustful eyes.

"You're not going to take him home yourself?" asked the second gendarme. "Can't you send someone else?"

"I'm going to take him to the parish house myself," the corporal replied. "He's worth that much to me."

He rode slowly off. A few people homeward bound followed behind, and behind them stumbled the bride's small sister. The second gendarme threw her a fleeting glance. She ran into a dealer's empty table, a few steps farther on upset a pyramid of tin cans and reeled against a sleeping donkey.

She's drunk, he thought. A pretty business, and still a child.

The bride's father and his sons stopped when they met the procession.

"You're going back to the cemetery?" the corporal asked. "Haven't you had enough of the fiesta yet?"

"I'm looking for my younger daughter," the bride's father replied. "You know her. Have you seen her?"

"She was standing in front of the cemetery watching."

"I'll teach her to behave like that," her father said angrily.

"Who have you got in that tarpaulin?" the younger brother asked. "Are you taking pity on a drunk?"

"That fellow's dead," said the corporal, nudged his horse and rode on.

"Who is it?" they shouted after him, but he did not hear them.

"It's Manuel from Marga-Marga," some of the people following him whispered. "And he has shot himself."

Neither the father nor brothers heard the muttering, for they had seen the little one and were running toward her.

The bride's little sister had not noticed the people talking with the corporal. Her eyes were riveted on the body lying across the horse's back. When her father suddenly thrust himself between her and the body she ducked. He struck her, but she made no sound.

XI

THE MOON SAILED ABOVE HIGHLAND AND CEMETERY, late drinkers shivered as they trotted out the gate, dogs got up and slipped away, their tails between their legs. The dawn wind put out the last of the candles. Gradually the shadow of the wall withdrew, revealing bride and bridegroom asleep in each other's arms beside the grave. There was dew on their poncho. A dog trotted up, sniffed at them and ran on. A flock of crows flew over them.

The trucks shimmered red in the rising sun. Recruits with boxes and bundles were streaming out onto the plaza, surrounded by their families. They looked at each other half solemnly, half timidly; they called greetings, smiled, nodded. The bride's two brothers were among them. They wore ties and had smoothed their hair with water. Their father and their small sister walked with them to the truck.

The groom's father and mother emerged from the twilight of a side street into the bright plaza. The old woman shrank back when she saw the trucks standing there. She had not slept that night, her eyes burned. In her fist was the medallion that carried all her hopes. She would emphasize to Pablo that he must never take it off, never, no matter what happened. He was an obedient son, he would do her this favor. But where was he?

The father was carrying a small cardboard suitcase that had cost a great deal, as much as a whole sheep. It was to be a surprise present. The groom had packed his things in a carton on the evening before All Souls' Day. During the night his father had transferred them to the new suitcase. On the inside of the lid, in big black letters, were written the groom's name and his home town. His father had had them inscribed a few days earlier by a monk from the parish house.

But where was the boy?

Here is something else for your trip, the father would say. No one has as handsome a suitcase as you. When the officers see it they'll treat you better.

He glanced over the other recruits' luggage. No, none of them had as fine a suitcase as this.

"He isn't here," the mother said in dismay.

"He's sure to be somewhere around," the father said. "The sun's already up."

"Have you seen Pablo?" the mother asked the bride's father.

"I thought he was with you, and with my daughter," the other said.

Nor had the two brothers seen him. No one knew where he was.

"He can't still be in the cemetery?" the mother asked,

more happy than fearful. "He wouldn't forget that he has to leave?"

Maybe, if he forgets all about it, they'll forget him too, she thought. And if they forget him, he can stay here!

"It wouldn't be good for him to miss the transport," the bride's father said. "I heard of a man who had to spend a couple of weeks in jail because he arrived too late for a transport."

"In jail he can't be killed," his mother said. "I'd visit him as often as I was allowed to, and take him food."

"You talk just like a woman," the groom's father said. "You don't understand about all this."

Oh, if only he doesn't come! she thought and was silent.

The howling of a dog woke Pablo. He emerged from the depths of a dreamless sleep, opened his eyes and saw a bright sky. He saw more: the top of the wall reddened by the sun.

He sprang up in alarm. The sun! He was supposed to be at the plaza by sunrise!

He glanced at Gorina, who was sleeping under the poncho and did not know he was no longer beside her. Hastily he spread the half of the poncho under which he had slept over her, and ran down through the empty cemetery and out the gate. He gave no thought to the drum. Scraps of paper were whirling in the air, dogs were digging in the rubbish heaps by the gate. A few hawkers still slept under their tables. Most of the carts and all but two of the donkeys had gone. On the roads that led from the cemetery out into the plain, the silhouettes of the last homeward bound stragglers shimmered in the morning sun.

Pablo ran. How far it was to Marga-Marga! So far, and the sun had already risen!

I'll get there too late! he thought. I have to go with them. O Madonna, let me get there in time.

He overtook two riders, the gendarmes. The corporal glanced wearily at him and recognized him.

"Aren't you one of those who have to leave today?" he asked.

"Yes," Pablo gasped.

"Oversleep?"

"Yes."

"Your wedding night. I can understand that," said the second gendarme.

"I'd be surprised if you got there in time," the corporal said. "They won't wait for you. They were due to start shortly after sunrise. The sun has been up for more than a half hour."

"They'll punish you," shouted the second gendarme.

"Lend me a horse," Pablo panted.

"We've had a hard night," the second gendarme replied. "We had a lot to do. The corporal rode to Marga-Marga and only got back a short time ago."

"I may not let this horse out of my sight except in a matter of life or death. You know it's no laughing matter for us to break regulations," the corporal said.

Pablo did not have the courage to beg one of them to ride on ahead. They could have asked the officer in charge of the transport to wait for another quarter of an hour, only ten minutes, a very short time, until he, Pablo, arrived. But perhaps the trucks had left long ago, perhaps he was running in vain.

Nonetheless he ran on, outdistanced the two horses and thought, I won't run to the plaza, but to the place where the road to Oruro leaves town. If the trucks haven't already passed there, I'll catch them. Then I can hail them.

The two policemen were now riding faster, but Pablo didn't notice.

"What are you going to do?" the second gendarme asked.

"Who knows?" the corporal said. "Perhaps they haven't left after all. We could save the poor fellow from being punished. Five minutes, after all, doesn't matter."

"They'll have gone."

"Maybe. But maybe not. It's worth a short gallop."

"That's you all over! Why do you bother about that boy? Why didn't he get up earlier?"

"Did you wake up at sunrise the morning after your wedding?"

"I didn't have to, thank God."

"Then you should feel sorry for him."

"Oh go to hell!" shouted the second gendarme. "If I feel sorry for anyone it's myself."

"Each according to his taste," the corporal replied.

Gorina felt for Pablo and found emptiness. She pushed the poncho from her face, sat up and looked around in amazement.

Was he at the fountain? She was cold. Clouds raced

over the cemetery; the grave wreaths chattered in the wind. She stood up.

Now for the first time she saw the sun over the wall, already high above the horizon. So Pablo had gone away and left her alone in the cemetery.

He didn't wake me up, she thought. He slipped away and let me sleep. Now I haven't said goodby to him or to my brothers. He could have taken me home with him. I would have run along at his side. He wouldn't have had to wait for me.

"Pablo!" she cried.

She wandered about among the screeching tin, the wind blowing through her hair, searching for her hat. But the dawn breeze had blown it over the wall and was now rolling it across the plain. Instead of the hat she found the drum. She drew it from under the poncho on which dew lay, turned it over so that the skin was uppermost and struck it timidly with her hand. She struck it again, more firmly this time, and then again, and then drummed on it with both hands and closed her eyes. Pablo was no longer there. She was alone in the cemetery with a few dogs and the drum and the stumps of candles on the graves.

But then she heard someone calling and when she turned around, hoping it was Pablo, she saw the old flute player. He was barely visible among the crosses. He was sitting in a ditch between two graves and beckoning to her.

"Have you seen Pablo?" she shouted.

"No. How could I see him? I've been asleep till now. Your drumming woke me up."

He got up and stumbled toward her.

"He's already on his way to the Chaco," he said. "Soon he'll send a letter. I'll go home with you to keep you company. But wait a minute, that fellow with the guitar's still asleep. I don't want to leave him here alone. He'll have one of his hangovers. I'll have to help him into town. That's the way he always is."

He ran to Uncle Lazaro's grave on his bandy legs.

But Gorina could not bear the old man, especially not on this morning. She kicked the drum away and ran toward the gate.

"Wait!" the flute player shouted after her. "I'm coming! Be patient!"

Gorina stopped and turned around but not because of the old man. She was frightened at the noise of the tin and the loneliness of the road home. So she ran back, picked up the drum again and carried it in front of her through the gate, beating on it wildly.

"Just wait, I'm coming!" shouted the old man. He tugged at the guitar player.

"Leave me alone," said he, but he suddenly leaped up: "Who's that beating on the boy's drum?"

"The bride."

"Go to her at once and tell her to leave the drum alone!"

He put his hands to his ears and threw himself full-length on the ground.

"Stop drumming!" the old man shouted down the hill. But Gorina could not hear him. She had already passed through the gate and saw on the far horizon the roofs of Marga-Marga. She threw the drum on a pile of old bottles and cans, the refuse from the booths, and ran toward the village.

"Martinez Cerda, Pablo!" cried the noncom who was calling off the list of recruits for the second time.

No one answered. The people craned their necks and peered about.

"They mean your son," said a man standing beside Pablo's father.

"I know, I know," he answered hoarsely.

"Hey, hasn't anyone any idea where he is?" the noncom cried.

Now they all looked at the father and waited for his answer.

"Are you his father?" the noncom asked.

"Yes, I am," the father said, bowing in embarrassment, and his wife standing behind him bowed even lower.

"Where's your son?"

"He'll be here any minute, he planned to be here by sunrise," the father stammered.

"I know, I know, the usual line: 'Where in the world can he be? Good God, if only nothing has happened to him. He was just here and now he's disappeared completely!' And we have barely left when he turns up, fresh and cheerful on the plaza and acts astounded that we are gone."

"But he promised us to be here."

"Don't worry, we'll find him, even if he isn't here now. Hardly anyone escapes us."

The father held up the new suitcase.

"We don't need the suitcase, we need the man."

"He'll be here right away," the mother cried. "He promised me. Why, I still have the medallion for him!"

"We won't wait for anyone," said the noncom. "He'll get his punishment, you can depend on it. That will be the reward, and he'll have to go to the Chaco just the same."

There was no one missing except Pablo. The noncom handed the list to a gendarme, who copied off Pablo's name. Orders rang out, the recruits sprang into the trucks, two noncoms ran about counting and cursing. Beside the officer in charge of the transport stood Don Eugenio, unshaven and with rings under his eyes. He was in uniform.

A whistle shrilled, the trucks began to move—three trucks full of recruits. The two brothers waved. Their little sister looked after them but did not wave back. With drooping shoulders and blank face, she stood beside her father.

"Sing!" shouted a noncom.

The recruits sang. Many of them did not know the song, but they opened their mouths and produced a few notes to make it sound louder. After all, one must obey.

The trucks drove once around the plaza. The boys' families stood sadly on the empty square and waved. A few women wept in their skirts. Then an alley swallowed up all three trucks, one after the other. The cloud of dust they had stirred up subsided, the song died away in the distance.

"And Pablo?" the mother asked.

Perhaps he's hiding somewhere nearby, so he won't have to go to the Chaco? Perhaps, now that the trucks had left, he would come out of his hiding place and would say: I'm staying here, Mother.

The father looked around helplessly; people were staring at him curiously.

The plaza emptied. Two riders approached at a gallop. Pablo's father saw that they were the two gendarmes who had spent the night in the cemetery. They rode straight across the plaza, threw a few words to the gendarme who was still standing there, saluted Don Eugenio and rode off. The father debated for a moment whether he should ask them about Pablo, but when he had finally decided to, they had disappeared.

"What are you going to do?" Gorina's father asked.

"I'm going to the cemetery."

"I'll go with you. My daughter will be with him."

"And I?" the mother asked.

"Take the suitcase home."

She nodded, picked up the suitcase and went off with it.

Oh, yes, Pablo had not gone away. The others had had to give up their young, but she still had him. O gracious Madonna of Copacabana, O dear Emilio, how kind you are! Now the medallion was no longer needed. She would hang it around the crazy one's neck.

The two fathers strode out of the town. The road to the cemetery was strewn with waste paper and donkeys' dung. The bride's little sister followed the men to the end of the town. There she turned aside and seated herself on the steps of the parish house.

"Go home," her father shouted to her.

"Yes, I will," she answered and stayed where she was.

When the men were half way they recognized Gorina running toward them from the cemetery.

"Do you understand this?" asked Pablo's father. "He isn't with her."

They both began to run.

Startled out of her sleep by the noise of the trucks, the crazy girl craned her head out the window. The recruits waved at her. She smiled mindlessly. The first truck went by, then the second, the third approached. Its noise reechoed in the empty alley. Among the recruits the red bird's head ruffled its feathers and laid its beak on the shoulder of one of the brothers. It gawked indifferently at the mad girl with half-closed lids. She leaned far out of the window and waved to it, for she knew it well; she liked it. But the truck disappeared in a cloud of dust. The crazy girl burst into hysterical laughter.

He has stayed here, his mother thought again and again, balancing the suitcase on her head. The nearer she came to her shack the faster she ran. Pablo would be home soon now, he could be there any moment.

From the other end of the alley a woman was waving to her. She stopped. Wasn't that the bride's aunt, wasn't that Uncle Lazaro's widow?

"Your Pablo was lucky!" she called.

"Wasn't he?" the mother replied. "I was so frightened, and then it turned out to be for nothing."

"You must have been sweating there in the plaza when he didn't appear."

"The non-commissioned officer was angry. He said he would punish him. But what does that matter?"

"That's a fine suitcase you have there."

"Yes, it's very fine, everybody looked at it."

"And what will you do with it now?"

"Oh, he'll need it sometime or other."

"But he hasn't even a poncho with him!"

The mother was confused. "Of course he has a poncho with him! Didn't you see him last night?"

Now the aunt was puzzled.

"I saw him climbing into the truck without a poncho."

"What truck?" asked the mother, alarmed.

"Why, the truck with the recruits, of course! Then you don't know that he stopped the trucks behind the last houses and got in?"

"My Pablo?"

"I looked out the window when I heard the trucks coming. I wanted to wave to my nephews. That was when I saw him running, all out of breath. He jumped over a couple of fences and waved to the trucks from a distance. The last one stopped, the boys pulled him in, and he was off."

"He's gone?" the mother cried, horrified.

"Didn't you know? I thought you must have heard by now. He was lucky."

"But the medallion!" the mother cried. "He isn't wearing the medallion!"

She opened her hand. The aunt saw the medallion, wet with sweat, and was terrified. This was bad.

"Why didn't you give it to him yesterday?" she asked.

The mother did not hear.

"He is not wearing the medallion!" she shrieked.

"Don't scream so," the aunt whispered. "Come inside and rest. Here, give me the suitcase. You still have it on your head."

But the mother turned away and reeled into the middle of the alley.

"He is not wearing the medallion!" she wailed.

A NOTE ABOUT THE AUTHOR

Gudrun Pausewang was born in 1928, of a German family, in a small town in Czechoslovakia. She was educated in West Germany, where she began her career as a teacher. After travels to England, Italy, and Spain, she lived and worked for years in southern Chile and Venezuela. Although she has been back to Germany to pursue academic studies and write, all of her stories are set in South America. Her first novel, *Rio Amargo*, was published in 1958. She published two others, one of which has been made into a film, before *Bolivian Wedding*, her first book to be translated into English, appeared in 1968. Since January 1968 she has made her home in Colombia.

A NOTE ON THE TYPE

The text of this book is set in Monticello, a Linotype
revival of the original Binny & Ronaldson Roman No. 1,
cut by Archibald Binny and cast in 1796 by that Phila-
delphia type foundry. The face was named Monticello in
honor of its use in the monumental fifty-volume Papers of
Thomas Jefferson, published by Princeton University
Press. Monticello is a transitional type design, embodying
certain features of Bulmer and Baskerville, but it is a
distinguished face in its own right.

The book was composed, printed, and bound by Kingsport
Press, Inc., Kingsport, Tennessee.
Typography design by Richard-Gabriel Rummonds
Binding and decorations by Paula Diane Silver